GUNS AT
BROKEN BOW

Center Point
Large Print

Also by William Heuman and available from Center Point Large Print:

Heller from Texas

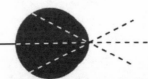

This Large Print Book carries the Seal of Approval of N.A.V.H.

GUNS AT BROKEN BOW

WILLIAM HEUMAN

CENTER POINT LARGE PRINT
THORNDIKE, MAINE

This Center Point Large Print edition
is published in the year 2019 by arrangement with
Golden West Literary Agency.

Originally published in the US by Fawcett Gold Medal.

The text of this Large Print edition is unabridged.
In other aspects, this book may vary
from the original edition.
Printed in the United States of America
on permanent paper.
Set in 16-point Times New Roman type.

ISBN: 978-1-64358-238-2 (hardcover)
ISBN: 978-1-64358-242-9 (paperback)

Library of Congress Cataloging-in-Publication Data

The Library of Congress has cataloged record
under LCCN 2019013351

GUNS AT BROKEN BOW

CHAPTER ONE

FROM THE RIMROCK here, looking down into the valley where the surveying crew was camped, Merritt Kane was positive of one thing. The surveyors for the railroad had not picked out the best route through the Yellow Hills, and he wondered about that, remembering from experience in Missouri how careful railroad men always were to select the course with the least obstacles so that the expense of grading and road building would be kept down to a minimum.

The gray horse was restless. Merritt watched the big gelding's ears twitch a few times, and then he threw away his cigarette and let the animal pick its own way down the shale to solid ground, and then to the grassy valley floor.

The surveyors' white-topped wagon was parked along the course of a tiny stream that meandered through the valley. White wood smoke drifted up lazily from their campfire. Three horses were tied in a little grove near the wagon. They had an army tent rigged up at the edge of the grove, and the campfire was crackling in front of the tent.

Moving leisurely across the flat valley floor, Merritt saw a man come out of the tent, stare steadily in his direction, and then go back into the tent and come out again with a rifle in his hands. A second man came out of the tent to stare at him, and then a third walked from the direction of the wagon.

Merritt's gray eyes flickered. He was a tall man, very loose in the saddle, with an almost thin brown face and high cheekbones. Under the black, flat-crown sombrero his hair was Indian black, inclined to be long. He had a Colt gun on his right hip, a hickory-handled gun, a very ordinary-looking gun, but the holster was different. The holster was of black leather, very smooth, well oiled, a trifle low on his hip because his arms were long.

His blanket was rolled in his slicker and tied behind the saddle. Coming in through the hills that morning it had been chilly, and he wore his coat, a short black jacket, faded in color.

The gray horse stepped across the gravelly bed of the stream, the water coming up to its hocks, clear, cold water running down from the hills. Riding up to the camp, Merritt waited for the invitation to get down. Although it was quite late in the morning, these three men were just having their breakfast. He could hear the bacon sizzling in the pan over the fire. There was the smell of coffee in the air, and it made him hungry again, even though he'd had his own breakfast less than an hour and a half ago back in the hills.

The invitation did not come. They stood there, staring at him as he sat astride the horse a half-dozen yards away, hunched a little over the pommel. They did not look like surveyors, either, even though he could see a surveying instrument standing near the wagon.

The man with the rifle in his hands was short and squat, with a cat's green eyes, a heavy growth of black whiskers on his face, and a flattened nose. The other two men looked as if they could have been hangers-on in a saloon. They were drab, nondescript men, staring at Merritt with vacant eyes.

"All right," the squat man grated. "What'll you have, mister?"

Merritt smiled at him. "Coffee smells good," he said. These men were touchy, afraid, and there was something wrong with that. Wherever it went the railroad was usually welcome, earnestly desired. These men were undoubtedly working for the railroad, laying out the route. He'd seen their stakes back in the Yellow Hills.

The squat man blinked once and then tightened his grip on the rifle. He said sourly, "Have a cup and move on, mister."

Merritt's smile broadened a little, and he shook his head. "Reckon I don't need it that bad," he observed. He sat there coolly, letting his eyes move around the camp, to the wagon, the tent, the tripod standing nearby.

The squat man rasped, "You seen enough now, Jack. Move that horse."

Merritt nodded. He didn't move yet. He started to roll another cigarette, and he looked down at them calmly. He saw the squat man's green eyes move to the gun on his hip, and to the Winchester rifle in the saddle holster.

"Passed your survey stakes back in the hills," Merritt stated. "I could have showed you a better place to cross that ravine a half mile back."

The statement caught the squat surveyor by surprise. His eyes widened a little and then narrowed. He said harshly, "You could, mister? An' who in hell asked you?"

The first flicker of real annoyance came into Merritt's eyes. He said softly, "Let it ride, friend."

The squat man had been going to say more, but he shut up now, recognizing the fact that there was a small warning in that casual suggestion.

"Nobody asked you to come here," the squat man said thinly. "Nobody's askin' you to stay."

Merritt looked down at him, smiling again, openly contemptuous now, and he didn't care if the man saw it. He walked the horse around them and left the camp on the other side, walking the animal past the white-topped wagon, giving it a steady, searching stare.

As he remembered this place, the valley narrowed another mile or two to the south after it had swung to the east a little. Coming up out of the valley he would hit into the stage road, running due south then and dipping into the draw, at the bottom of which lay the town of Broken Bow.

He'd come through here seven years before, and he'd never forgotten the town. As marshal and sheriff of four different hell-on-wheels boom towns during the past seven years, he'd thought of Broken Bow many times, and always in the back of his mind had been the thought that he would come back someday; that he would settle in Broken Bow, buy some land, run a little stock, become a decent, useful citizen, maybe even marry and raise his own children.

That was the dream, and looking at it now, only a few miles from his destination, he wondered why he had waited so long. They'd paid him big money in Ellsworth, in Brisbane, in Abilene, in Cairo City to walk the streets with the gun on his hip, to use it when he had to, to wear that bright shining star on his chest. He hadn't done it for the money, because no amount of money was worth the eternal vigilance a law man had to maintain in a town where the law was hated and despised, and where there were always a dozen men ready to shoot him down from a darkened alley each and every night of the year.

He'd taken these jobs because there was a feeling inside him that they had to be done, that someone had to do them, and that the profession called for certain qualifications. He had those qualifications. He'd never stopped to analyze himself and to ask where he'd got them from, or why he was obligated to use them. It was enough that he was qualified to uphold the law, to carry the big gun, to wear the star.

Now it was Broken Bow, after seven years, and the dream still strong, and he was only thirty-one. He rode the gray horse around the bend in the valley, started the big animal up the slope, and then stopped when a rifle cracked from a point halfway up the slope.

He heard the lead whine over his head. He saw the light puff of smoke drift up from a clump of brush about two hundred yards ahead of him. Stopping the horse, he sat there, making no move to dive for cover, the cigarette in his mouth, hands holding loosely the horn of the saddle.

He sat there for nearly a full minute, just looking at the spot from which the gun had been fired. It had been a Winchester. He could tell that from the peculiar detonation, high and sharp.

Then he started to ride forward again, smoking the cigarette, letting the gray horse just walk up the slope directly toward the ambush. The Winchester cracked again, this time the bullet coming lower, almost touching his hat.

The gray horse kept going up the slope, oblivious of the bullets, as oblivious as its rider. Coming to within twenty-five yards of the hiding place, Merritt could make out a figure crouching there, the barrel of the Winchester poked through the brush. Those shots were intended to frighten, but not to hit.

Another bullet whizzed by his head, but he kept riding, smoking the cigarette, never stopping until he was within fifteen feet of the rifleman, and then he sat there, staring.

A girl was coming out of the brush, the rifle in the crook of her arm, her face white with rage. She wore faded blue jeans and a gray flannel shirt. Her dark-brown hair was tucked in under a black sombrero. Her eyes were deep blue, in strange contrast to the color of her hair.

She said tersely, "You have your nerve, mister."

"Reckon you have some yourself, ma'am," Merritt told her. "The women all carry Winchesters in this country, and take pot shots at strangers?"

"Some of us carry bull whips, mister," she snapped, "and we use them on prowling skunks."

Merritt grimaced a little. He flipped away the cigarette, and he sat there, arms folded across his chest, looking down at her quizzically. Then he said, "You see me ride out of that surveyor's camp, ma'am?"

"Of course I saw you," the girl grated. "Why do you think I tried to stop you?"

"You didn't shoot low enough," Merritt smiled. "Lose your nerve?"

"Turn around and come up again," the girl said ominously. "We'll see."

Merritt shook his head. "Hate like hell to ride up to a nervous woman with a gun in her hands," he observed. "Sooner walk into a rattlesnake's den." He saw the anger blazing up in her eyes again, and he deftly changed the subject. He said, "Why put a bullet through a man who's done nothing more than ride through a railroad surveyor's camp?"

The brown-haired girl stared at him steadily. "You're with that outfit," she accused.

"Ever see me before?" Merritt asked her.

She bit her lips and then shook her head.

Merritt said gently, "Reckon you could be wrong, lady. Now, why don't you want a railroad through here?"

The girl scowled, but she was not sure of herself now. She said crisply, "How did you know I don't want a railroad?"

Merritt shrugged. "You're holding up the surveyors," he pointed out, "and the surveyors work for the railroad. That means you don't want the road. Why? The railroad brings prosperity to a place."

"Prosperity and hell," the girl snorted. "Haven't you ever seen a railhead, mister?"

"Railhead?" Merritt repeated. "They figure on making Broken Bow the railhead?"

The very thought of the thing made him a little sick. The railhead was the end of the track, the terminus for this particular branch of the road.

He'd seen what had happened to other sleepy little cow towns when the railroad came to them and stopped. Passing through, the steel rails brought prosperity, a way to ship away surpluses, and a way to bring in needed commodities cheaply. When the line stopped in the town the same conditions applied, but that was not all.

The end of the track meant cheaper commodity goods, but it also meant that every tinhorn gambler, every footpad, every big gambling-house operator, every cheap dance-hall girl, and every saloonkeeper within a radius of two hundred miles flocked to the town to set up quarters. He'd seen that happen in Abilene, in Ellsworth, in other towns where the steel tracks had been run and then stopped.

Within three months after this railroad came to the quiet little town of Broken Bow his dream would be shattered. The chances were that the transformation had already started to take place. They would be battling in Broken Bow for the choice corners and building lots. Land speculators would be rampant, grabbing everything in sight, paying little to the unsuspecting townsmen, selling at enormous profits when the rails came into sight.

The end of the track in many instances became the end of the town, also. The steel rails split the town into two factions. The decent people remained on one side of the track, and the bad element on the other. In the course of time one or the other would predominate, and he'd seen that happen; he'd been in the middle of conflicts like that. In Cairo City the bad element had won out. They'd taken over control of the town, electing their own crooked officials, and in time the decent people had moved out, and then the town had died because it had no substance. Rotten to the core, it had died its hideous death, and Cairo City was still there, the end of the track, with the rusted steel rails edging out across the open plains, stopping now in a ghost town.

Merritt Kane said slowly, "You're sure about that, ma'am?"

"Great Kansas is building south and west," the girl said grimly. "The surveyors are within three miles of the town now. After the surveyors come the grading crew, and then the rails."

And then hell on earth, Merritt thought bitterly, with decent people afraid to step outside their doors at night; with men being knifed in back alleys, with young trail riders losing a month's wages on the turn of a crooked card, with possibly crooked law men to enforce crooked laws, and pale-eyed killers, their guns for hire.

Merritt said absently, "I'm not with the railroad, ma'am. Just rode through that camp. They didn't even ask me to light for a cup of coffee."

The girl was looking at him curiously. She said, "We've been holding them down in the valley

16

there. I thought you were one of them, coming through to make trouble. I'm sorry."

"You won't stop a railroad with a Winchester," Merritt told her. "A railroad is big business, power, money, influence. They'll run over you if you get in their way."

"On the other hand," the girl said tersely, "they might grow discouraged if there's enough opposition, and head some other way, bypassing us."

"That's a thought," Merritt nodded. "How strong is this opposition in Broken Bow?"

"None of the ranchers want the road," the brown-haired girl said. "I own Double Bell, one of the smaller outfits around Broken Bow, but I can speak for the larger ones, too."

"Double Bell," Merritt murmured.

"I'm Sabine Bell," the girl half-smiled. "Dad worked out the Double Bell brand thirty years ago when he came to this country."

"I'm Merritt Kane," he answered. "Always figured ranch men wanted the railroad," he said curiously. "Where's the advantage running cattle up to another railhead, Miss Bell? They lose flesh and you lose dollars."

"We've figured that angle of it," Sabine Bell nodded, "but we've been moving our stock up to Beaumont, two hundred miles to the north, for the past fifteen years. It's not much of a run, and we've found that our stock doesn't lose enough weight on the trail to make any real difference. On the other hand, with Broken Bow the railhead, every rancher in the territory would be running his stock up here, and besides that, there are still plenty of Texas longhorns coming up the trail. They'd make this range their final bedding ground, and they'd try to build up the stock run down on the trail."

Merritt nodded, getting the point now. He'd seen this thing happen, too, and it was not always pleasant for the ranchers in and around the railhead.

"You spread thirty thousand head of cattle here," Sabine Bell finished, "and where do we come in? There's not that much grass and water for everybody."

She'd turned and started to walk back to the thicket where her horse was tied. When she came back, leading the animal, a little sorrel, Merritt said to her curiously, "Thought you were guarding this end of the valley, keeping those surveyors from coming through."

Sabine tossed her head contemptuously. "They won't do any work this late in the day," she said.

Merritt watched her step into the saddle. She rode like a boy, lithe body swaying with the movements of the horse, and she turned the animal up the slope and onto the stage road that led to Broken Bow.

Over her shoulder, Sabine Bell said to him,

"Looking for a job? I can always use a few more riders." She said it carelessly, but she was listening for his reply.

Merritt smiled faintly. "Reckon not," he said. The last place he wanted to stay now was Broken Bow. There would be no peace and quiet in the town. The storm was gathering over the little cattle town, and the peace he'd once anticipated was vanished. It was as if a great cloud had come over the town, blotting out the sunshine.

Sabine didn't make any comment, but he could tell from the set of her head what she was thinking. He was a drifter, turning down a steady job, wanting no part of this trouble coming to Broken Bow. She had her contempt for him—a woman's contempt for the shiftless.

Chapter Two

AT HIGH NOON, Broken Bow lay asleep at the bottom of the draw, and there was not too great a change in it since Merritt Kane had passed through seven years before. There was a long, straggly main street with a half-dozen intersections. There were fewer gaps between the houses than there had been, fewer vacant lots. The side streets seemed to run farther east and west.

The white steeple of a church lifted up against the deep blue of the sky, and that was new. They had a bridge across the tiny rivulet that cut across the entrance to the town, where before there had been a few wooden planks.

Beyond the town the road lifted up out of the draw again, disappearing through a cut in the slopes to the south. From the top of the draw Merritt could see every section of the little town, every house, every moving thing.

The northbound stage was swinging down the slope now, just entering Broken Bow, leaving behind it a banner of dust. A buckboard was moving down the main street slowly, the two chestnut horses in the traces just stepping along. Out in front of one of the saloons a swamper was pushing his broom along, stopping to look

21

up as the stage tore around a slight bend in the road, a dog or two racing along with it, barking excitedly.

Merritt said thoughtfully, "A nice town, Miss Bell."

"We like it," Sabine Bell nodded.

There was a schoolhouse up on the slope, a rough-board, one-story building with a flagpole in front of it, and a flag hanging limply in the still air. Merritt had the odd thought that when he passed through here years before, this girl riding at his side had been in that schoolroom studying her lessons.

They went down the slope, their horses clumping across the bridge, and then they were on the main street. Merritt remembered a hotel; he remembered the stage office and the depot where the stage was now waiting. There were many more saloons now than there had been, an indication that the town was growing already. He noticed at least a half-dozen new buildings going up along the main street alone, another indication that Broken Bow anticipated a boom of some kind.

At this hour there were not too many people stirring. It was hot down here at the bottom of the draw at this hour of the day. Later in the afternoon, Merritt remembered, a cooling breeze swept in from the north, traversing the entire draw, chasing away the hot air, giving the town cool, comfortable nights.

Two men sat on the porch in front of the Comanche Saloon, looking at them curiously as they rode by. One man touched his hat to Sabine Bell, and she nodded.

Diagonally across from the Sherman Hotel at the main intersection was another new building, a one-story affair with a false front, shining in its new white paint, the only building in town painted. There was a big glass window in the front of the building, and in gilt letters on the window the words "Paramount Realty Company." In smaller letters below the company title were the words "Stephen West."

A tall man in black stood just outside the entranceway to the building, his hands in his back pockets, watching them come down the street. Merritt had noticed him about to turn the doorknob and step into the building. Then he'd stopped to watch them.

As they came up, the tall man in black took a cigar from his vest pocket, bit off the end, and put the cigar in his mouth. He did not light it. He stood there, the cigar tilted a little toward the sky, smiling, a handsome man with golden-brown hair, a wide, clean-shaven face, a deep cleft in his chin. His eyes were pale blue, the eyebrows very light, almost blond.

He was neatly and cleanly dressed. His shirt was white and of excellent material. He wore a string tie and a beautifully embroidered vest, a light gray in color. Nodding, he said to the girl, "How are you, Sabine?"

He was looking at Merritt, though, sizing him up, looking at the horse, at the gun on Merritt's hip, at the condition of his clothes, rather threadbare and dusty after a month on the trail.

Sabine Bell had edged her horse over toward the store, and she slowed down now, and she said, "Those surveyors are still in the valley, Stephen. They haven't come any farther than they were last week. I took a shot at one of them, or rather someone I thought came from their camp." She glanced at Merritt slyly.

"Poor shooting," Merritt murmured. "She missed three times."

"She wouldn't have missed," Stephen West observed, "if she'd wanted to hit you, my friend."

"Merritt Kane," Sabine Bell introduced them. "Stephen West—my fiancé."

It came to Merritt as a distinct shock, although he could see no conceivable reason for it. For all he knew, this girl could have been married, but it was still a shock. His gray eyes flicked, but his face showed nothing.

West came out to the edge of the boardwalk and held out his hand. It was a big hand, strong, smooth, uncalloused. Merritt shook it. He said, "Glad to know you, West."

Stephen West said, "Staying in Broken Bow, Kane?"

"If you are," Sabine Bell grinned, "he'll sell you a piece of real estate in fifteen minutes."

Merritt glanced at the new building behind the real-estate man. He said thoughtfully, "You seem to be doing pretty well, West."

Stephen West's pale eyes narrowed very slightly, but he was still smiling blandly. He said, "Broken Bow is a growing town. When the railroad gets here it will really boom."

Merritt wondered at this. Sabine Bell did not want the railroad; she and the ranchers of Broken Bow were already fighting it, but she was engaged to marry a man who would stand to make much profit when the rails came through.

Sabine Bell said, as if reading Merritt's thoughts, "Stephen and I differ about the railroad. He feels that he's taking the more practical view."

"You can't hold up the wheels of progress," West smiled. "If it's coming, it'll come. If not this year, why, the next, or the year after that, but it'll come."

"Then it's good business," Merritt said, "to buy up plenty of land before the tracks get here, and before the crowd begins to come." He could have added, And sell it at a hundred-per-cent profit.

Stephen West was smiling up at him, rolling the unlighted cigar in his mouth. There was no smile in his eyes. He said, "Good business sense, Kane." He let it ride like that, and then he said,

"You expect to be around when the road gets here?"

Merritt remembered that he hadn't answered the man's question about his plans in this town. He said now, casually, "Hard to say."

"If you do," West murmured, "stop in and see me. We might be able to do some business." He dismissed Merritt with that remark, and he said to Sabine, "I'll be up at the Goodman property late this afternoon, Sabine."

"Stop in for supper," the girl nodded. "I'll expect you."

They moved away from the walk, and Merritt edged over toward the hotel, looking up at the building. It was two stories high, a rambling rough-board structure with a porch running across the entire front, a long hitching rack at the edge of the boardwalk.

"I'll put up here," Merritt said.

"Only hotel in town right now," Sabine told him. "A new one will be going up on the next block as soon as the railroad comes in sight."

"Mr. West sell them the property?" Merritt asked idly.

The girl glanced at him. "That's right," she said.

There was a faint smile in Merritt's eyes, but he didn't make any comment. He wondered, though, how much profit the smooth Stephen West had made on the transaction. He wondered

26

quite a bit about Stephen West, and about Sabine Bell, too, knowing now why the girl had fallen for him. In Broken Bow there would not be too many men like West, men with polish, education, background, poise, and the looks to go with them. In the eyes of Sabine Bell, West was an astute businessman, rising in the world, and a man who would be a power in this town when it grew up.

"On your way out," Sabine said, "you'll pass Double Bell. We're a mile and a half to the south. Stop in if you change your mind about that job."

"I'll think about it," Merritt smiled. "Thanks."

He dismounted in front of the hitching rack, slipped his saddlebag from the saddle, and slung it over his shoulder. He watched Sabine ride on to dismount in front of a dress shop down the street, and then he ducked under the rail and went up on the porch.

A thin, half-bald clerk with spectacles said, "Plenty of room right now, mister. Won't be when the rails get here."

"That right?" Merritt murmured. "And when will that be?"

The clerk shrugged. "They ain't started building yet," he said. "Takes time for a railroad to come through."

Merritt stared at the desk, at the book in front of him. Then he wrote his name in the book, but he was still thinking that it was queer the railroad hadn't even started to build yet. Usually, the graders came right after the surveyors. He'd assumed all along that the graders were back somewhere on the other side of the Yellow Hills, leveling the right of way. The fact that the road had not even been started, and already new buildings were going up in Broken Bow, was an indication that the town had already jumped the bell.

"Heard there was a new hotel going up in town," Merritt said as he put the pen down.

"Be plenty of 'em," the clerk said, "and profit for all. Old Man Andrews bought the Messner place. Tore the old house down, and he's bringing in lumber now to build."

"Stephen West sell Andrews the Messner place?" Merritt asked.

"He did," the clerk nodded. "West bought it from John Messner six months ago."

"For a song," Merritt said. "He didn't sell it for a song now, did he?"

The clerk grinned at him. "West is a business-man," he said. "He'll do well in this town."

"Reckon he will," Merritt murmured. He had one more question for the clerk, and he thought he could risk that without seeming too curious about West. He said, "When did this talk start about the railroad coming here?"

The clerk thought for a moment. "First time I heard about it was after the last snowfall we had—middle of March."

Merritt figured back. It came to five months,

and West had been buying property for six months, possibly longer. He wondered whether it were possible that Stephen West had inside information about the road coming to Broken Bow, and was cleaning up now.

"Road's coming," the clerk was saying glibly. "Surveyors are out in Spring Valley now."

"They tell me," Merritt said, "that the ranchers don't want the road."

The clerk took a key from the board behind him, slapped it on the counter, and said, "Those that stand to make profit want it; those that don't, don't. That's about the size of it." He added tersely, "But it's coming, mister. Ain't no power on earth can stop the railroad."

Merritt didn't say any more. He went up to his room, placed his blanket roll on the chair, and looked at his reflection in the cracked mirror above the bureau. He needed a haircut, and he needed a shave, but worse than that, he needed a bath.

Locking the door, he went downstairs again, stabled the gray in the livery stable behind the hotel, and crossed the street to the barbershop. The barber, a short, fat man, dozed in the chair. When the door opened and the bell jingled, he awoke with a start.

Merritt said, "Warm water ready, friend?"

"Be ready," the barber grinned, "after you've had a haircut and shave, mister."

Merritt unbuckled his gun belt, slipped off his coat, and sat down in the chair. When the chair was tilted back a little, he lay there while the barber busied himself in the back, setting the big kettles of water over the stove. He was not quite certain now what he would do. Broken Bow was definitely not the place in which he wanted to settle. He told himself that he would stay here a day or two and then move on, probably somewhere to the south and to the west. It did not matter a great deal where he went.

The barber bustled back into the room, humming to himself. Merritt said to him, "Slow afternoon."

"Won't be," the barber grinned, "when the road gets here, friend. Hear about it?"

Merritt frowned. "Heard about it," he said briefly, and he was rapidly becoming tired of hearing about it. Broken Bow had become railroad conscious. It was probably the only topic of conversation among the men.

The barber went on, "Everybody figured Great Kansas would bypass us and build up to Junction Center. That's a hundred miles to the north. Changed their plans then, and now they're movin' this way."

"How much track is laid?" Merritt asked.

The barber posed in front of him, his scissors in his hand. He repeated, "Track?"

30

"Steel rails," Merritt said patiently. "How much track has Great Kansas laid?"

The barber grinned. "Haven't started to build yet, mister," he explained. "Takes time to build a railroad, you know. Surveyors are here. They've laid the stakes through the Yellow Hills already. Graders should be comin' through in a few more weeks. You'll see hustle around here then, mister."

Merritt didn't say anything. He sat in the chair, staring into the mirror as the barber clipped his black hair. Something was disturbing him. He could not yet make out what it was, but somewhere, somehow, something was wrong here. He hadn't liked the surveyors in Spring Valley; he hadn't liked the route they'd picked through the hills. Not a surveyor himself, he was positive he could have selected a better route.

He did not like Stephen West either, and he wondered for a moment if this was because West was engaged to Sabine Bell, and was making himself a small fortune in real estate in this town.

He was disgruntled, too, because he'd made his own plans as far as Broken Bow was concerned, and now those plans were shot through because the steel rails were coming out to the town.

"Saw you ridin' in with Sabine Bell," the barber was saying. "Friend o' the Bells, mister?"

Merritt scratched a hair away from his cheek

31

where it was itching him. He said, "How many are there?"

"Just the two of 'em," the barber told him. "Sabine and Roxy."

"Roxy?" Merritt murmured.

"Roxy's nineteen," the barber grinned. "Kind of a hellcat in these parts, mister."

"I see," Merritt said.

"Wanted to get married when she was fifteen," the barber told him, glad to have news to impart. "Young feller up on the Slash C. Sabine stopped that. Stopped a lot of Roxy's nonsense. Sabine's smart. Runs Double Bell like a man. They're makin' money out there. First time since her father died."

"I hear Sabine's marrying Stephen West," Merritt said, and he let the barber play around with that statement as he knew the man would. A barber was a man who heard a lot of things because he saw a lot of people, and if he was the kind of man who could not keep information to himself, he would be bubbling over like a pot, ready to give it away.

"Stephen West," the barber said with satisfaction. "Now, there's a man, mister."

"That right?" Merritt said dryly.

"Come here less than seven months ago," the barber went on. "Already has his own building, and makin' plenty in real estate. Must own half o' Broken Bow already, and he'll own all of it when the road comes here." He added mischievously, "Not only that, mister, but he hooks the nicest girl in these parts. Half the loose riders on this range and all the unattached businessmen in town are dyin' of envy."

Merritt thought of that—of the first part of it. West had been in Broken Bow only seven months, and already he was being regarded as one of Broken Bow's top citizens—a solid, substantial businessman who was out to make his fortune on the railroad.

Sabine Bell, who evidently was a good businesswoman, would appreciate a man like that, who in a comparatively short time had established himself. She did not appreciate drifters. He'd noticed that.

The barber stopped clipping for a moment to look out through the window as a rider shot by on a little blue roan. The rider was hatless, black hair flying in the air, long black hair in braids. The rider was a girl, in a white blouse and faded blue jeans. Even before the barber told him, Merritt knew who she was—the fatherless and motherless Roxy Bell.

The barber said, "Roxy Bell. Someday she'll ride that damn horse right off the bridge an' kill herself. Reckon she's comin' in now to see young Jonathan."

"Jonathan?" Merritt repeated, and he let the barber work on that one.

"Jonathan West," the barber said. "Stephen's brother. Musician. He's supposed to be kind of sweet on Roxy."

Merritt moistened his lips. "Double wedding," he said, "at Double Bell."

The barber laughed uproariously, but Merritt's grin was sardonic. He said, "Jonathan in the real-estate business too?"

"Hell, no," the barber said. "Jonathan ain't in much of anything. A musician, like I said. Plays the piano like a wizard. Just hangs around, watchin' everything, everybody. Don't do nothin'."

"Reckon Stephen does enough for both of them," Merritt observed, and he was a little surprised at this revelation. In one family there was a crafty, energetic businessman and a shiftless artist. He wanted to meet this Jonathan who played the piano like a wizard, and sat around doing nothing, just watching.

He had his shave and he had his bath, and when he came out on the street the sun had lost some of its heat, and the breeze was beginning to sift in from the north end of the draw.

Hungry now, he crossed to the hotel restaurant and had his meal at one of the corner tables. He was thinking of Stephen West now, probably out at Double Bell having his supper with Sabine Bell. From his position in the dining room he could look out across the street and see the West

34

realty office. The door was locked and the office was empty.

After supper he went out and sat in a wicker chair on the porch. There were more people around now. Riders were coming in, tying up at the various hitching racks along the street, heading for the saloons. The late-afternoon sun gleamed red on the big window of the Paramount Realty Company across the street, and then dusk came to Broken Bow.

Merritt Kane lighted a cigar and sat there, listening to the sounds, the talk, watching the people. A beer wagon had pulled into the valley next to the Wide Open Saloon, and they were unloading. Two old men were engaged in a mild argument outside the closed doors of the Broken Bow Bank, a short distance down the street.

Then he heard the piano, the music coming out over the batwing doors of one of the saloons down the street. Merritt Kane listened, his eyes wide in amazement. He'd heard piano players in these towns before. Nearly every honky-tonk had one—a drunk who picked up beer money pounding out the popular tunes of the day. The barber had called Jonathan West a wizard, and Merritt had assumed he was better than the ordinary run of honky-tonk piano players.

The man playing the piano down the street was not a honky-tonk player. He was playing music, real music, classical! It was a beautiful piece, soft and yet lilting, ideally suited for the hour of the day. It was the kind of music that could make a man dream.

It went on and on for fully ten minutes, and then it ended in a beautiful little finale. Merritt Kane threw away his cigar and stood up. He wanted to meet Jonathan West—another drifter.

CHAPTER THREE

THE WILD WEST SALOON was the biggest one in town, and already at this early evening hour there were a dozen or so horses at the rack. Merritt spotted several bearing the Double Bell brand, Sabine's riders. There were other brands here, too. He counted three of them—Slash C, Hatchet, T-Rail.

The saloon had a long bar, and the bar was about half filled. Pushing through the batwing doors, Merritt saw first the man at the piano in the corner of the room. He sat with his back to the bar, a rather thin man in black, bareheaded, his hat resting on the top of the piano. He had his brother's hair, but it was an even lighter shade, almost honey-colored.

His hands caught Merritt's eye. The piano player reached for a glass of beer on the piano, and Merritt saw the hand—long, slim, white, with tapering fingers, the fingers of an artist.

A big, heavy-set man in a black derby stood at the end of the bar, cracking his knuckles as he leaned over the wood. He was the bouncer for this house, probably an ex-pugilist. Merritt had seen too many of them to be mistaken. The bouncer had a wide, bony face, a battered nose, heavy black eyebrows. His hands were huge, misshapen, and he stood there, cracking one knuckle and then the other, watching everything and everyone.

His eyes swiveled to Merritt as Merritt came up to the bar. He had brown eyes, and they were not bad eyes, but they seemed wholly out of place in that face.

He nodded to Merritt, recognizing him as a stranger, and he said, "Enjoy yourself, Buck."

"Aim to," Merritt smiled. He pointed to a bottle on the shelf, and the bartender took it down, slid a glass in front of him, and moved away.

The bouncer edged over. He said, "Railroad man?"

He was even bigger than Merritt had thought at first. He wore a short jacket, much too tight for him, and his huge hands and wrists protruded from the sleeves. He wore an oilcloth bow tie that snapped a little as he came around the edge of the bar.

Merritt smiled at him, liking him. He said, "I've ridden on the railroad, friend. That's all."

"Big Sam," the bouncer introduced himself. "Big Sam McGee. Forty-eight rounds with the Benicia Boy. Broke both hands."

Merritt nodded to the bottle in front of him. "Drink with me," he invited.

"Never touch it," Big Sam smiled. "Bad for the stomach. Now, English ale. There's a drink, friend. Works like a tonic. Got to like it in London.

Fought against the best of 'em in London—bare knuckles."

He had a staccato way of speaking, one sentence following the other with scarcely a pause for breath.

He said, "Great little town, Broken Bow. You'll like it, friend. When the road comes through it'll boom. Might not be so good then. We'll see."

"We'll see," Merritt nodded. He saw Jonathan West getting up from the piano stool, moving toward the bar. West was young, not more than twenty-one or -two, tall like his older brother, but not as heavy in the shoulders. He had blue eyes like Stephen, too, but they were a darker shade of blue. His honey-colored hair was inclined to curliness.

He came to a stop at the bar about three or four feet from where Merritt stood, and Merritt turned slightly and said, "You make that piano talk, Mr. West."

Jonathan West grinned boyishly. "Thanks," he said.

"Met your brother this afternoon," Merritt continued. "I'm Kane, Merritt Kane."

"Glad to know you, Mr. Kane," Jonathan said. He accepted the drink Merritt pushed toward him.

Big Sam had edged around the corner of the bar again, and was standing there in his accustomed place, watching everything, smiling at customers, cracking his knuckles. Each night the ex-fighter stood here, preserving the peace, handling recalcitrant drunks, a small god in a little world. He seemed to like his work.

Merritt turned his attention to Jonathan West. He said, "A man with your ability should be studying to play in the concert halls of Europe. Why hide here in Broken Bow, Mr. West?"

Young West shrugged. "Stephen came out here," he said. "I came with him." It was a simple statement of fact. It was as if he had no brain or will of his own. He went with his brother. If Stephen entered hell itself, Brother Jonathan would follow unhesitatingly.

Merritt pondered over this fact as he sipped his drink, and then he heard the raucous shouts out in front of the saloon. Horses had pounded up the street, coming to a stop in front of the Wild West.

Big Sam was looking toward the batwing doors, a frown coming to his face. He looked at Merritt and scowled.

"Hatchet riders. Must o' had a few in Milltown before comin' in here. That means trouble."

The Hatchet riders, six of them, stormed through the doors, nearly tearing them from the hinges. They were pretty big men, their faces shining, flushed with the liquor they'd already consumed before riding into Broken Bow. It was still quite early in the evening, and as the night wore on there would be more of them present, making the rounds of the Broken Bow saloons.

The leader of this group from Hatchet seemed to be a big red-haired, freckle-faced man in a calfskin vest. As they moved up to the bar he was the man who came in contact with Jonathan West, jostling him rudely, nearly spilling the liquor from West's glass.

Young West reddened a little and edged away from the group. He did not have a gun, and Merritt could see that a man of his physical powers would stand very little chance against anyone in the room. Jonathan West did not belong here.

Big Sam McGee was still cracking his knuckles, a little more loudly than before, eying the Hatchet riders. They'd ordered their drinks, downed them, and now they were looking for fun. Several of them moved over to a card table, kicked back chairs, and sat down.

The big redhead stood at the bar, both hands on the wood, swaying a little. He was looking straight at Jonathan West in the bar mirror, and Merritt, watching him, saw the grin spread across his face.

The redhead said, "If it ain't the Professor! Play us a tune, kid."

Jonathan West had turned slightly pale. He stood there at the bar, licking his lips, and then he shook his head. "Not tonight," he said.

The redhead was grinning at him. Merritt saw

him put a hand in his pocket and come out with a coin. He dropped it on the bar in front of Jonathan West, and he said softly, "Play us a tune, kid."

Other men were listening in on this now, grinning a little. Jonathan West was afraid, but again he shook his head, and Merritt admired the young man for it. He was in for a thrashing and he knew it, but he wasn't crawling. He could very easily have gone over to the piano, laughing off the incident, played something hastily, and then got out. He stayed where he was at the bar, looking down at the coin on the wood.

"Play us a tune," the redhead repeated, his voice ominous now.

Sam McGee cleared his throat. He called across the bar, "Easy, Kramer."

Kramer slid a Colt out of the holster at his side, placed the weapon on the bar, and said, "McGee, this ain't your affair. I ain't fightin' you with fists. You hear?"

"I hear," Big Sam murmured. He looked at the gun on the bar, a pearl-handled Colt .44. He didn't like the looks of it.

Red Kramer took Jonathan West by the arm, spun him around, and sent him lurching in the direction of the piano.

"Something nice, Professor," he grinned.

Merritt Kane said, "That's far enough, Red."

The redhead had seen him on the other side of West, but had taken no particular notice of him.

42

He stood against the bar now, resting one elbow on the wood. He said softly, "How'd you get in this, Buck?"

"Walked in," Merritt smiled. "Let that boy alone."

Red Kramer studied him thoughtfully, his eyes moving down to the gun on Merritt's hip, up to Merritt's face, to his left hand resting on the bar, and then back again to the gun. He said to Jonathan West out of the corner of his mouth, "You gonna play, kid?"

Young West stood about a half-dozen feet away, backed up against one of the chairs near an empty card table. He was very pale now, and he was breathing heavily. Merritt could read his thoughts. He wanted to run away, to get out of this, but he didn't want to be laughed at.

Casually, Merritt reached his hand along the bar and picked up Kramer's gun as Kramer watched him, mouth open. He broke the gun, pushed the cartridges out, placed them in a neat little pile on the bar, and then slid the gun back toward the redhead.

Kramer cursed and then stepped forward to retrieve the cartridges. As he did so, Merritt put out a hand, placed it against the redhead's chest, and pushed.

A man at the door yelled at the top of his voice, "Fight—fight!"

Kramer swung a roundhouse right for Merritt's

head, but he was wild with the punch, and Merritt moved in swiftly, smoothly, ripping his left hand into the redhead's stomach, doubling him up. As Kramer's head went down, Merritt's right knee came up, catching him across the forehead. He went down in the sawdust on the floor, gasping for breath, mouth open, but he was not finished.

The other Hatchet men had got up from the card table nearby, and they were watching grimly as Kramer got to his feet, rubbing his stomach.

Sam McGee called to them warningly. "Two men make a fight, boys. No more. You hear me?"

Red Kramer tore in, face pale with anger, swinging wildly as he charged, and Merritt backed away coolly. The redhead's greenish eyes had an unnatural hue. They seemed to give off sparks.

Merritt hit him in the mouth with a left fist, but still kept retreating carefully toward the wall behind Sam McGee. When he reached the wall, he put both hands back against it and catapulted off, driving hard into Kramer, hitting savagely at the man.

He saw Jonathan West watching him. He saw the crowd coming through the doors of the saloon, yelling excitedly, forming a smaller and smaller circle around them.

A Hatchet man called tersely, "Get him, Red!"

Red was staggering back through the crowd, trying to protect his face from the hailstorm of blows coming at him. He was bleeding from the nose and from the mouth now, but Merritt kept after him, giving him no respite, hammering.

As he followed Kramer through the crowd, a boot came out, ramming against his right ankle, tripping him. He lurched against one of the tables, his head striking the wood violently, and he went down, stunned. Another boot came at him, the tip of it catching him under the chin, driving his head up, putting him flat on the floor.

He could hear a man yelling, "Hatchet! Hatchet!" It was the rallying call. Then he heard Sam McGee's booming voice, "Off him—off him!"

He got up to a sitting position again, conscious of the whirl of legs around him, unable to do anything. A boot came down across his fingers, bruising them badly, and he pulled the hand away. He could hear the blows, hard, heavy, like the sound of a butcher's cleaver striking the chopping block.

A man lay on the floor beside him, holding his mouth, blood spurting through his fingers, rocking back and forth, moaning. Then another man came down, his body striking the floor with a sickening thud. He lay beside Merritt, twitching.

Merritt looked at the big legs in front of him, the black, tight-fitting pants and jacket. The shoes were eastern shoes, black leather, square-tipped. He watched the shoes shifting around on the floor, and he listened to the thud of those murderous blows, and then another man came down beside him, a man who collapsed as if all the bones had been suddenly taken from his body. He lay that way on the floor.

Big hands grasped Merritt under the armpits, hoisting him up, sitting him on a chair. Sam McGee said concernedly, "You all right, Mr. Kane?"

Merritt's head was still throbbing, but the ache was going away now. He sat on the chair, looking ruefully at his bruised knuckles, and then rubbing his chin, which had become very tender. He watched the Hatchet riders dragging the three beaten men to a back room, and then he saw Red Kramer's head above the crowd on the other side of the room. Kramer was still a little dazed, daubing at the cuts on his face with a blue handkerchief, shaking his head.

Jonathan West came over to Merritt, bent down a little, and said quietly, "Thanks, Mr. Kane. I didn't want you to get in trouble over me."

"No trouble at all," Merritt grinned, trying to be nonchalant. He almost fell off the chair.

Big Sam came back with a glass from the bar. He held the glass to Merritt's lips and Merritt drank the liquor. He felt better when he got up.

Sam McGee said, "You look all right now, Mr. Kane."

Merritt stared at the big man critically. He said, "How many rounds did the Benicia Boy go with you, Sam?"

"Forty-eight," Sam said.

"How did he last that long?" Merritt smiled, and he clapped the big bouncer on the back.

Through the crowd still in the room he saw Stephen West pushing his way from the door. A smaller man followed West, a man with a bright, shining star on his vest, and Merritt found himself staring at the little man, trying to place him, positive that he'd seen the sheriff of Broken Bow before.

The man with the star was thin-shouldered, thin-faced, with a stubby nose, ash-blond hair, and small, close-set amber-colored eyes. He had long arms for a small man, and very small, delicately formed hands. The big Navy Colt on his hip looked enormous beside the boyish hand.

The two of them came over to the table at which Merritt sat, and when the small man saw Merritt he stared, eyes widening, and then his brown face became bland again. Merritt was quite positive that this man had recognized him, too, but he still could not place the sheriff. Somewhere, a long while back, he'd run across this man, and he should have remembered him.

Stephen West said quietly, "Heard you stepped in for my brother, Kane. Thanks."

Merritt didn't see Jonathan West in the room.

He looked up into West's wide, strong face and he said, "They wanted to rough him. He seemed like a nice boy."

"They won't rough him any more," West said tersely. "They won't try that again." It was the big brother speaking now, meaning what he said.

Merritt got up from the chair, rubbing his chin a little. He said quietly, "This town is no place for him, West. You know that."

"I know it," Stephen West murmured.

The sheriff had pushed on through the crowd, and Merritt saw him talking with Red Kramer. West went away, looking for his brother, and Merritt stepped over to the far end of the bar, where Big Sam McGee had taken up his position again, his big shoulders hunched.

"Who's the sheriff of this town?" Merritt asked curiously.

McGee nodded in the little man's direction. "Finn Tragan," he said, and then as an afterthought, "Stephen West got him the job after George Neill went to California."

"West?" Merritt murmured. "He's a pretty big man in this town for a fellow who's been here such a short while."

"Smart man, West," Big Sam agreed. "Very smart. People around here think a hell of a lot of him."

"I've noticed that," Merritt said, and he started to think of Finn Tragan. The name meant nothing to him, so it was very possible that Tragan had changed his name. Many men did that in this territory.

Looking over the batwing doors a few moments later, Merritt saw Sheriff Tragan talking earnestly with Stephen West outside on the porch. The yellow light from the interior of the saloon revealed their faces quite clearly. Tragan was nodding toward the saloon doors, speaking vehemently. Then the two men moved away out of Merritt's sight. He was quite positive they'd been talking about him, and he was quite sure that someone in Broken Bow knew who he was. He hadn't intended to talk about that.

Walking down the street toward the hotel ten minutes later, Merritt saw two people standing close together at the darkened corner across the road from him. A door opened near them, throwing lamplight across them for a brief moment, and Merritt recognized the two as Jonathan West and Roxy Bell, the wild girl of Broken Bow. He wondered that these two, so utterly opposite, should have fallen for each other, and he realized bleakly that this was another factor that would draw Stephen West and Sabine Bell together. She undoubtedly worried about Roxy, and she would like to see the girl settle down.

Young West, while having a reputation in Broken Bow as an idler, was as good a catch as Roxy could make, and Jonathan West would always have his brother behind him, steadying him, pushing him if need be. Sabine would know that.

Merritt went up the steps of the hotel and into the lobby, feeling of his tender chin, and he was amazed at the number of people he'd met this day in Broken Bow. Some he'd liked very much; some he did not like. He told himself that tomorrow he would be thirty miles away from it, away from the railroad troubles to come, away from this impending double wedding in Broken Bow, which somehow was annoying him. He should have been happy with this thought, but strangely enough he was not.

Chapter Four

AT EIGHT O'CLOCK the next morning Merritt was a half mile out of Broken Bow, the big gray horse anxious to run. They were already passing groups of Double Bell stock grazing on the slopes. This was good cattle country. He'd noticed that before. The grass was excellent, and there was plenty of water. The cattle were sleek and contented, and they stared at him curiously as he went by.

He passed the Double Bell ranch, remembering Sabine Bell's invitation to him to stop in if he changed his mind about work. He remembered, too, the veiled contempt in her eyes when he assured her that he was not looking for work. That thought gnawed at him a little now, and he did not like it.

Double Bell was a log affair, low, with an additional wing spreading out to the west. It had a veranda that looked very cool, overgrown with vines.

The bunkhouse was fairly large, and they had a good, substantial corral in the rear. He could see a Double Bell man inside the corral, snaking out a mount.

White wood smoke curled up from the chimney of the main house, and Merritt had his picture of the two girls having their breakfast, Roxy Bell thinking about Jonathan West, and Sabine thinking of the day's work; perhaps, too, of Stephen West.

On the other side of Double Bell the land started to rise, and then after topping a rise a mile from the ranchhouse it dipped again. It became more wooded here, with great parks in between the stands of timber. He'd always liked this kind of country.

There was water, plenty of it; a lake, a stream running into it, good grass. Far to the west he could make out the foothills of the Rockies, lifting up above the long grades of the western plains.

More cattle grazed in these open parks, and Merritt read the brand on them—Running G. Running G was Double Bell's neighbor. He wondered how it would be to live next to Sabine Bell, to drop in occasionally; to exchange the time of day and small stock news.

Five minutes later he came upon Running G headquarters, an unimposing place, considerably smaller than Double Bell, half hidden among the cottonwood along the stream that trickled here.

The corral was old and in need of much repair. It was empty at the moment. Someone was home, because smoke came out of the chimney. The bunkhouse for the Running G riders was quite small, too. There were a few sheds, one of them having fallen to pieces.

Moving up closer, Merritt read the sign, a shingle nailed to a tree. It read, "Arch Goodman."

Merritt stared at the shingle for a moment, and then he remembered where he had heard the name Goodman before. Stephen West had mentioned that he would ride out here yesterday afternoon. He wondered if it were possible that West had come here to buy the Goodman place. A bell started to tingle inside Merritt's head. Very possibly Arch Goodman was trying to sell this ranch! It was exactly the place he would have liked to buy if he had remained in Broken Bow.

He looked at the house with interest, and then at the corral and the other buildings, his mind moving rapidly. The place could be repaired without spending too much money, and Arch Goodman had the range here, water, timber, everything a man wanted.

As he sat there, staring at the shingle, a rasping voice came from the porch. "Get off that horse, mister, an' have a cup o' coffee."

It was an old man's voice, a snarling old man who pretended to be meaner than he was. Merritt saw him standing at the edge of the porch in his undershirt and suspenders, gray hair sticking up in tufts, a thin, gnarled old man with skinny arms, a wedge of a face, and pale, deep-sunk blue eyes.

Smiling, Merritt dismounted and walked up to the house. The old man turned and went inside without saying another word, Merritt following him, his boots making the porch boards squeak.

In the kitchen the old man was bent over a wood stove. Merritt said to him, "Arch Goodman?"

"That's right," the old man growled. "Sit down. Coffee's about ready. Damn if I ain't sick o' eatin' alone."

Merritt sat down at the kitchen table, grinning a little in spite of himself. Goodman brought the coffee over in an unclean cup, black coffee as thick as cream, with a powerful odor to it. He had a cup for himself, but he didn't sit down. He stood a few yards away from Merritt, sipping the boiling hot coffee, and he said, "What brings you up this way, mister?"

Merritt looked at him as he stirred the coffee aimlessly. He took a long leap, knowing that he was doing wrong. He said, "This place for sale, Mr. Goodman?"

Arch Goodman looked at him suspiciously. "How'd you know?" he demanded.

"Heard Stephen West was up here," Merritt told him. "I figured it that way."

"Damn all the Wests!" Goodman exploded. "Damn all real-estate men who buy for nothin' an' sell for a fortune!"

"That's right," Merritt nodded.

"Why in hell do you want to buy?" Goodman

demanded. "Railroad's comin' in here, young man. Every damned rancher in the county is afraid the road'll ruin him."

"Didn't say I wanted to buy," Merritt observed.

"Why'd you ask if you don't want to buy?" Goodman grinned slyly. "It's for sale, if you're askin'. I'm headin' for California. Damned rheumatism. I need sunshine, dry air."

"How much did West offer you?" Merritt heard himself say.

Goodman named the figure, and it was ridiculously low. He said, "Why ain't you worryin' about the railroad, mister?"

"I could fence it in," Merritt said, "if I had to. It'll come to that anyway in time out in this country."

"Fences!" Arch Goodman exploded. "Time to get out. Make your offer, mister."

Merritt looked at him. He thought of Sabine Bell, of Broken Bow, of Stephen West, and of the railroad, and then he named a figure—five hundred dollars higher than Stephen West's.

Arch Goodman's grin broadened. He held out a calloused hand, and he said, "You're in business, mister."

Merritt took the hand. He drank the coffee and he got up. He said, "Meet me at the bank in Broken Bow at two o'clock this afternoon. I'll make out a draft for you on an Omaha bank. I'll have a lawyer."

"Damn all lawyers," Arch Goodman said, but he was grinning. "See you, mister," he said.

Merritt rode back the way he had come. He rode slowly, asking himself why he had done this, why he was inviting trouble for himself. He liked the land, but there were troublesome days ahead. The fence he'd mentioned to Arch Goodman might get him into a lot of trouble with other ranchmen in the vicinity, even though it would protect him from the trail drivers coming up to the railhead. They liked free range in this territory, and the first man to put up a fence was sticking his neck out.

Being Sabine Bell's neighbor was another matter, and it could have been a very nice matter, except for one thing: Sabine was engaged to Stephen West.

He had to pass the Double Bell ranch on the way back, and this time he turned down into the valley, riding straight up to the door. A Double Bell rider sitting on the corral fence saw him and lifted a hand. Merritt heard him say to a man inside, "That's the feller took Red Kramer last night."

Sabine Bell came out on the porch when she heard his step on the wood. She was wearing a dress now, and she looked different. It was a blue dress with white trim, and it brought out the color of her eyes. She looked at him, smiled a little, and said, "Change your mind, Mr. Kane?"

56

Merritt shook his head, and he saw the small annoyance come into her eyes. She frowned at him, and he had the feeling that she was disappointed.

He said, "Passing by, Miss Bell. Thought I'd drop in for a neighborly call."

"Very nice of you," Sabine said ironically, "even if you're not a neighbor."

Merritt glanced back at the sun, squinting a little. He said, "Will be about three o'clock this afternoon."

Sabine Bell's eyes widened a little. "What's going on?" she asked curiously.

"Bought the Goodman place this morning," Merritt told her. "I get title this afternoon."

Sabine was staring at him. Roxy Bell came out on the porch behind her sister, a slightly taller girl, her hair darker than Sabine's. She was quite beautiful in every sense of the word, long, dark lashes, violet eyes. She reminded Merritt of some wild creature of the forest.

Sabine said, "Roxy, this is Mr. Merritt Kane, our new neighbor. He's buying the Goodman place."

Roxy smiled, revealing beautiful teeth. She said, "Much nicer than Arch Goodman, I'd say."

Merritt grinned at her, liking her the way he would like a young cub. He noticed that Sabine flushed slightly, and he wondered why.

Sabine said, "I'll have to show you the boundaries of our respective ranges someday, Mr. Kane. I don't suppose Arch bothered."

"I have an idea how much land I have," Merrittt said, "but the ride wouldn't hurt me any. We'll have to get together someday."

Sabine frowned a little because Roxy was grinning openly. Changing the subject abruptly, she said, "I suppose you'll think differently about the railroad now, Mr. Kane."

Merritt shrugged. "Reckon I'll wait till the road comes," he observed. "Never liked to kill a chicken till I was ready to eat it."

Roxy Bell said curiously, "You sound as if you weren't too sure that the railroad would come here, Mr. Kane."

"It's supposed to come," Merritt nodded. "I'll wait for it. I'm here now."

"Anything we can do," Sabine said, "as neighbors, let us know."

Merritt smiled a little. As he turned to go, he said over his shoulder, "Nice to have good neighbors." He heard Roxy's tinkling laugh as he went back to his horse.

At two o'clock that afternoon he met Arch Goodman in front of the bank, and he had the town lawyer, Martin Stone, with him. Stone was a fussy little man with spectacles, unable to stand still very long. When Goodman came up, he bustled both of them into the bank, and as they went through the main entrance of the red-brick building, the only brick building in town, Merritt saw Stephen West coming out of the office of the president. He saw the words painted on the door just before West opened it: "Asa Creel, President."

Creel came out with West, pausing just outside the doorway to say a few more things. He was a thin little man with narrow shoulders, bent inward. He had large ears that stuck out from the sides of his nearly bald head. His eyes were small and beady, reminding Merritt of a rat, and they kept moving around from side to side, taking in everything.

West saw them coming in, and he watched them curiously as they went over to one of the windows. He didn't notice Arch Goodman at first, but when he did, Merritt saw the reaction in his eyes.

West came over to them when Creel went back into the office. He nodded pleasantly, and he said to Goodman, "What brings you to town, Arch? Still thinking of selling your place?"

"Sold," the old man grinned triumphantly, "to this here chap, West. We're transferrin' title now."

Stephen West looked at Merritt, and this time he could not hide the dislike in his eyes, even though he continued to smile. He said, "Heard you were riding on, Mr. Kane. What made you change your mind?"

Merritt shrugged. "Liked the looks of the Goodman place," he stated casually. "Maybe I'm playing a hunch."

Stephen West took out a cigar and lighted it. He rolled the cigar around in his mouth, and then he looked at the floor. He said gently, "Let's hope you're lucky, Mr. Kane. A man needs luck in this country."

He nodded then, and he walked out onto the street. Martin Stone was saying, "All right, all right. Shall we go to my office now?"

The transfer was made in less than an hour, and Merritt came out of Stone's office with the deed in his coat pocket. He had about 150 head of cattle on the property, and the stock was included in the transaction.

The old man said, "Reckon you'll find Tom Morse in town somewhere, Kane. Tom's been helpin' me around the place when I need him. He'll go along with the deed. Tom's like that."

"I'll look him up," Merritt nodded. He shook hands with the old man, and Goodman promised to be packed and out in a few days. "Straight for California?" Merritt asked him.

"Allus wanted to see Chicago," Goodman grinned. "Takin' the stage east first. California next."

Merritt located Tom Morse in the Comanche Saloon. Morse was a tall, lank man, his long arms hunched around a glass of beer at the bar. He had a cavernous face and deep-sunk, smoky blue eyes. Shaking hands with Merritt, he said, "Glad to see that old cuss get out. I'll work for you, Kane."

Out on the street again, walking toward the hotel, where he would have to register again for tonight, Merritt spotted Big Sam McGee hustling toward him, grinning broadly, holding out a huge ham of a hand.

"Heard you bought out Arch Goodman," McGee chuckled. "Glad you're stayin' in Broken Bow, Mr. Kane. You'll never regret it."

"Let's hope not," Merritt smiled. He added, "News gets around in this town, Sam."

"Arch dropped into the Wild West before meetin' you at the bank," McGee explained. "He's been shootin' off a little."

As they talked they were standing directly in front of the sheriff's office, and Merritt glanced toward the window. It was dusty, dirty, but he could see inside. He could see Finn Tragan sitting behind the desk, his boots up on the top of it, hat thrust back on his head, as he looked out the window straight at the two men standing there.

Merritt turned his eyes away from the window, giving no indication that he'd been able to see

Tragan through the dirty glass. Again, he was positive that he'd seen this man before, and under unsavory circumstances. Someday he would remember.

CHAPTER FIVE

THERE WAS A DANCE that night in the Roseland Dance Hall. Merritt heard the talk in the hotel dining room as he ate alone early in the evening. He read the poster tacked to the wall near the door on the porch.

After a while, sitting on the porch alone in the dusk, he heard the band tuning up down the street. Buckboards and lone riders were already moving in from the back country. These dances were quite special events, staged by the Cattlemen's Association, and they were not held too frequently.

He remembered that he was part of this now, part of Broken Bow, and part of all its activities. As a cattleman he eventually would be enlisted in the association. He would get to know his neighbors. He would raise his stock, engage in spring and fall roundups, try desperately to care for his stock in the winter with the rest of them, sweat, worry, and freeze through the winter, hoping that he would not lose too many head, and then begin again in the spring.

All this would be very nice if the railroad did not smash the dream to pieces. He would have to wait and see about that. If the cattlemen of the territory were strong enough, they could do something about the trail herds encroaching on their ranges; if the decent citizens of Broken Bow stood on their rights, they could do something, too, about the tinhorns coming in. In the meantime he could wait and enjoy this period of peace and quiet.

A half-dozen riders tore down the main street, headed for the dance hall, whooping, kicking up showers of dust. There were more buckboards, some of them jammed with children; mothers carrying babies and basketsful of food, coming in to have supper here, having spent two and three hours bouncing along rutted roads to reach the town.

Merritt saw Jonathan West and Roxy move past on the opposite side of the street, walking arm in arm, and it was a nice sight. Again he was amazed at the paradox of Jonathan and Stephen West.

After a while there was only a lone rider, spurring down the street, coming in a bit late, reluctant to miss any of the fun, and then another buckboard rolling slowly, with two people in it.

Merritt saw the cigar glowing in the darkness as the man on the buckboard smoked. As they drew opposite the hotel, he heard Sabine Bell's soft laugh and Stephen West's voice.

They didn't see him sitting in the shadows, and the buckboard moved past. Merritt listened to the wheels crunching the dust, and then he put his boots up on the railing, staring across the street at nothing in particular. It was getting very quiet at this end of town. The saloons were almost empty, practically all of the men having gone on up to the Roseland.

Merritt Kane's lips were pursed, and he experienced a vague dissatisfaction. He was restless tonight. Possibly the sight of Sabine and West going to the dance together had affected him, even though he knew that it should not have. They were engaged, and he'd been aware of that thirty minutes after he first met Sabine. If he'd had any ideas in that direction, he was foolish even to consider them.

He tried to concentrate upon the fact that he'd come to this town for peace and quiet, and at this moment he had his peace and quiet. It was not enough. He stirred restlessly in the chair, and then he heard the squeak of shoes on the walk, and only one man in Broken Bow wore eastern shoes instead of boots.

Sam McGee said, "You a dancin' man, Kane?"

McGee was smoking a cigar, and he stood there just below the railing, in the shadows, looking at Merritt.

Merritt said, "You don't dance by yourself, Sam."

The bouncer nodded. He pushed his derby hat back on his head a little. "Lots of women comin' in from outside," he observed. "Quite a few you ain't met in this town, my friend."

Merritt shrugged. He'd never been too much interested in women in recent years, because he'd had to concentrate upon just staying alive in some of the towns where he'd upheld the law. He'd met women, but they'd meant nothing to him, and then he'd met one in this town of Broken Bow who possibly could have meant a lot, but she belonged to another man, and it was the way of the world.

"Comb your hair," McGee advised. "Put on a clean shirt an' join the fun. You belong here now, man."

He went on then, the cigar tilted toward the night sky, a simple man, a man who was a king in his own little world, the Wild West Saloon; a man who was liked and respected by those who knew him. Merritt Kane wondered if this should not be enough for every man. McGee had no great problems. He did the kind of work he liked to do, and the work for which he was best fitted. He did not seek fame or fortune, and the peace of mind other men sought long and desperately and unsuccessfully he already had.

Merritt sat there for some minutes, listening to the music down the street, listening to the laughter. After a while he got up and moved to the edge of the porch and stood there. Then he turned and went up to his room.

He had a clean shirt in his bag, one he'd never worn. He took it out, shook out the wrinkles as best he could, smoothing it down, and then he put it on. He combed his hair before the mirror, and he looked at his reflection. McGee, of course, had been right. There *were* other women in this town, and he was a solid and respectable citizen. As a citizen of Broken Bow he was supposed to participate in its social activities.

There was the usual crowd of men around the doorway when he came up. Inside he could see the dancing couples, and the orchestra up on a stand at the far end of the room. Colored paper lanterns had been strung across the room, and it was decorated with colored paper streamers.

Sheriff Tragan was talking with a few men to the right of the entranceway. He turned and looked at Merritt as he pushed his way through the crowd.

A dozen little boys chased around the corner of the dance hall, yelling excitedly, still full of pep, but the very small ones sat on their mothers' laps in the chairs just off the dance floor, sleepy-eyed.

There was the usual stag line along one wall of the long, barnlike building, but Merritt didn't go over to it. He saw Sabine and Stephen West out on the dance floor, Sabine smiling happily, and he felt a little stab of pain go through him.

The dance floor was filled. Grinning, red-faced punchers swung their partners around. The musicians up on the stand sawed away on the fiddles and plucked the guitar strings.

Merritt located the familiar, friendly face of Sam McGee, and moved over that way. McGee stood alone, still chewing on his cigar, leaning against the wall to one side of the floor.

He smiled and nodded when Merritt came up, and he said, "Only a fool sits by himself on dance night, Merritt. Enjoy yourself."

Merritt looked at him, and then leaned against the wall next to him, hooking his fingers in his belt. He'd checked his gun at the door as he went in.

Jonathan West and Roxy moved past, and they saw him. Jonathan nodded and smiled. Roxy looked at him, sizing him up and down, and then her eyes moved out toward Sabine at the center of the dance floor. The young couple slid by.

Sam McGee said, "Nice people. That Roxy is a good girl. Had a few wrong ideas years ago, but Sabine got her through it."

"That's nice," Merritt murmured.

"That Sabine Bell," McGee said. "There's a girl."

Merritt didn't say anything. He'd heard that before, too. He was thinking grimly, Do they have to rub it in?

Sabine Bell and Stephen West were coming their way now, and Sabine saw him against the wall as she swung around. She nodded and smiled. She said something to West, and he glanced in Merritt's direction—casually, almost too casually. He was a good dancer; he was a man who probably did everything well, and who succeeded in whatever he was doing.

McGee said, "You ain't a bad-lookin' man, Merritt. Plenty o' girls here would like to dance with you."

"All right," Merritt said, but he didn't leave the wall, and McGee looked at him and shook his head.

After a while the music stopped and the dancers left the floor. Many of them stepped outside for a breath of air. It was quite hot in the building.

Sabine came directly toward Merritt, Stephen West moving along behind her. She stopped in front of him, and she said, "I see you are becoming a real citizen of Broken Bow, Mr. Kane. As a member of the Cattlemen's Association, I'd like to welcome you."

"Thanks," Merritt nodded. He looked at West, and West was smiling. He'd never liked a man who smiled that much when there was nothing to smile about.

West said, "Been out to look over your place yet, Kane?"

"Saw it already," Merritt said briefly. "It won't change in one day."

"That's right," West chuckled. "You made a good deal for yourself, Kane. Planning on joining the association?"

"If they'll have me," Merritt nodded.

"I'll put you up for membership," Sabine told him. "You're a neighbor."

"Nice to have good neighbors," West almost purred. The remark was not addressed to Sabine, but to Merritt. He was looking straight at Merritt as he spoke.

Merritt said, "It helps."

"Enjoy yourself tonight," Sabine smiled. She was looking straight at him as she said it.

Merritt nodded. "Aim to," he told her.

They went away, and Sam McGee stirred restlessly against the wall. "Had been me," he said, "an' I'd o' asked her for a dance. She was waitin' for that."

"How do you know?" Merritt asked him.

McGee shrugged. "I'm a man don't do much," he said. "I stand around an' I listen. I watch things goin' on. After a while a man like that gets to know."

"You could be wrong," Merritt said.

"Even if I was," McGee grinned, "wouldn't hurt none to ask her."

"I'll dance when I'm ready," Merritt told him.

"When you're ready," Sam McGee observed, "it might be too damned late, my friend."

Merritt didn't say anything to that. He pushed

away from the wall and he headed for the outside, moving through a side door. There were lanterns out here, too, illuminating one side of the building.

Beyond in the shadows the buckboards were drawn up, and Merritt could hear a baby crying. There were a few tables here, and some of the families were enjoying a late-evening snack. A group of punchers in the shadows down near the end of the building had a bottle, and they were passing it around.

Couples drifted by, talking in low tones, waiting for the music to begin again. Merritt rolled a cigarette, lighted it, and stood by himself, his back against a tree.

A man said to him softly, "So you're goin' into ranchin', Kane."

Merritt turned his head slightly, and looked at Sheriff Finn Tragan. Tragan was smoking a cigar, standing with his feet apart, hands stuck in his back pockets, the cigar tilted slightly.

"That's right," Merritt said.

Tragan nodded. "Good business in this part o' the country," he stated. "A man can make out." His face was in a poor light, and Merritt couldn't see it clearly. Tragan said, "Done a lot o' ranchin', Kane?"

Merritt turned a little more to face him now. "Some."

Tragan murmured, "That's the way it is. A man

71

does this, an' he does that, an' then he thinks he'll raise some cows an' take it easy. That how it looks to you, Kane?"

"That might be," Merritt observed, and he had the strange feeling now that Tragan knew him, too, and that he was maliciously jesting.

"Best o' luck," Tragan said, and again there was that hint of a jest in his voice. He moved off, Merritt watching him go, and then a girl came up and stood directly in front of him.

It was Roxy Bell, and she said grimly, "Why didn't you ask her for a dance, Mr. Kane?"

Merritt blinked. "Who?" he asked.

"My sister," Roxy snapped. "How old are you, anyway?"

"Old enough to still give you a good spanking," Merritt smiled. He added, "Your sister seems to be occupied, Roxy."

"She's not married yet," Roxy scowled, "and I hope she doesn't marry him."

Merritt thought about that for a moment, and then he said, "Why not? Everybody in this town seems to think well of Stephen West. You like his brother."

"Jonathan and Stephen live in two different worlds," Roxy told him tersely. "They're different people."

"What have you got against Stephen?" Merritt asked curiously, wondering where and how these two had crossed.

Roxy shook her head and looked at the ground. "I don't know what I have against him," she admitted, "but I just wouldn't like it if he married Sabine. Maybe it's womanly intuition."

"Maybe," Merritt murmured. He found himself hoping fervently that Sabine wouldn't marry West.

"Stephen came to this town when there wasn't anybody else around," Roxy said grimly. "Or would you consider Arch Goodman somebody? What do you expect her to do?"

"I don't know," Merritt said.

"They're engaged," Roxy told him, "but they're not married. Keep thinking about that, Mr. Kane."

"I'll think about it," Merritt murmured.

"But you'll stand out here," Roxy said tersely, "or you'll lean up against the wall inside, but you won't do anything. I know your kind."

Merritt didn't say anything. He stared at this intense girl, wondering at her anger, and then realizing that it was because she loved her older sister, and that perhaps in many ways she was wiser than Sabine. Sabine knew cows and she knew horses, but she could be mistaken about men because she'd been so busy maintaining the ranch that she hadn't had time to learn about men. When a man like Stephen West came along, she reacted as any young, inexperienced girl would. Roxy seemed to be aware of that, and she'd detected a flaw in that smooth marble front of Stephen West.

"Ask her for a dance," Roxy urged. "That's not hard to do. This is a public affair, and you're a neighbor. She almost expects that."

"All right," Merritt said. There was no evading this girl; there was no way to put her off.

"I'll ask her for you if you're afraid," Roxy grinned. "I'm not really mad at you, Mr. Kane. It's just that I saw you standing there against the wall, not looking at anybody else but Sabine. I think I know how a man feels when he looks at a girl like that. I want to help."

"Much obliged," Merritt told her.

"Much obliged," Roxy mimicked. "Bah!" She strode away, and Merritt smiled after her.

The music had started up again inside, and he pushed away from the tree, taking a deep breath as he headed for the door. He spotted Stephen West and Sabine chatting with two other ranchers up along the right wall.

Jonathan and Roxy were just moving out on the dance floor, and Roxy gave Merritt a grim look. Sam McGee was watching, and McGee nodded as Merritt went past him up in the direction of Sabine Bell. He came up at her right side with West's back toward him, and Stephen West didn't see him until he was speaking with Sabine.

Sabine had turned and was smiling at him, he

hoped expectantly. He said, "As a neighbor, Miss Bell, I was wondering if you would care to dance with me."

Sabine's smile broadened. "You don't have to be a neighbor to ask for a dance in this part of the country, Mr. Kane," she said.

West turned around, a stub of cigar in his mouth. He nodded pleasantly, but there was a glint in his eyes. Then he went on talking, but as Merritt moved out on the floor with Sabine Bell he felt West's eyes following them.

"I'm rusty," Merritt apologized. "Reckon you'll have to watch my boots, Miss Bell."

"I didn't imagine a man like you did too much dancing," Sabine laughed. "What did you do before you came here, Mr. Kane?" Then she caught herself, and she shook her head before Merritt could make any kind of reply. She said, "I had no right to ask that question. I should have known better."

"I did a little of this," Merritt murmured, "and a little of that."

Sabine grinned at him. "I could have asked it," she said.

She danced very well because she was light on her feet rather than because she was an experienced dancer. They moved away from Stephen West and the ranchers, and out on the center of the floor they passed Jonathan and Roxy. Roxy nodded to him and winked gravely.

Merritt said, "Your sister and young West make a nice couple. How serious is it?"

"Serious as can be," Sabine told him. "I guess Roxy's old enough to know what she's doing now, and I like Jonathan. He hasn't found his proper place in life yet, but he will someday. He's not a drifter, and he has a tremendous amount of musical talent."

"Good luck to both of them," Merritt nodded. Then he added, looking over her head, "Good luck to you."

"Thank you," Sabine murmured. She didn't say too much after that, and eventually Merritt steered her back to West.

He didn't dance with her again that night, but he did dance with Roxy at her request, and the girl asked him quickly, "Well?"

"Well what?" Merritt wanted to know.

"You make a date with her?" Roxy demanded. "Did you ask to take her riding some after-noon?"

"No," Merritt said.

Roxy took a deep breath. She said slowly, "Cautious or afraid, Mr. Kane?"

"Neither," Merritt stated blandly. "Too late."

He walked home alone that night after seeing Sabine Bell and Stephen West drive off in the buckboard. He walked slowly down the street to the hotel. The dance was breaking up. The music had stopped. Some of the riders were drifting into saloons along the street; others had taken the trail back to their bunkhouses.

Sam McGee, coming up behind Merritt, said, "A very nice evening, Merritt."

"That's so," Merritt nodded. He watched Stephen West's carriage moving along up past the hotel, taking the stage road south out of the draw. As he paused in front of the hotel for a last word with McGee, Jonathan West and Roxy came up and were moving past them.

Merritt said, "My gray could use a little exercise, Jonathan."

"Thanks a lot," Jonathan nodded, gratitude in his voice.

Roxy called back over her shoulder as they went past, "If you were a man, Mr. Kane, you'd be using that gray yourself tonight."

Merritt smiled wryly in the darkness as he rolled a cigarette, and Sam McGee said curiously, "What'd she mean by that, Merritt?"

"She's a strange one," Merritt stated. "She has a sense of humor." He felt kind of flat, though, himself, as he went up to his room.

Chapter Six

WITH TIME ON his hands the next afternoon, Merritt rode north out of Broken Bow, the gray clumping across the bridge, heading up the slope and out of the draw. He wanted another look at that route the railroad surveyors had staked through the Yellow Hills, and he wanted another look at the surveyors themselves.

As he reached the summit of the draw, the northbound stage whirled past him in a cloud of dust, the driver yelling a greeting to him as he went. Skirting the valley in which the surveyors' camp was located, he moved due north into higher ground.

The Yellow Hills were a series of low mountains, sparsely covered with vegetation, and having from a distance a yellowish color. The country was rough, cut with ravines and deep gullies. The stream that cut through the valley wound in and out among the hills, and in the course of two miles Merritt had to cross the same stream three times.

He picked up the stakes he'd seen a few days before, and he followed them, studying the route carefully, and as he progressed deeper and deeper into the hills, following the stakes, he became more convinced that this route had been picked almost at random. The railroad had to go through the hills to reach Broken Bow, but it would have been much easier to route the tracks farther south where the slopes were not so precipitous, and costly bridges and trestles would not have been necessary in many instances.

At the top of a bluff he sat astride the gray horse, rolling a cigarette, looking down at a number of wooden stakes hammered into the ground on either side of the stream. It was another bad crossing, and for the road to go through here there would have to be much blasting, much excavating, and another costly bridge.

He was convinced now that either the surveyors for the railroad were terribly incompetent or they did not particularly care where the tracks were laid. And it was hardly conceivable that a railroad would hire incompetent surveyors to lay the route, in as much as in their hands lay decisions that might cost the line huge sums of money.

Some distance behind him he distinctly heard loose shale slide down a slope. He sat there, staring down at the stakes, listening carefully, and then he lighted the cigarette and rode on again, quite sure now that he was being followed.

He rode on leisurely, let the gray pick its way down the slope to the stream, followed the course of the stakes another quarter of a mile, and then, leaving the stakes very abruptly, he swung around a low hill, climbed the hill, and approached the summit very carefully. He sat there, looking down at the course he'd just traveled, and in a few minutes a rider came along. He was astride a big chestnut animal, moving forward cautiously as he came.

The sun glinted on something shiny on his vest, and Merritt Kane knew that the man following him was Finn Tragan, sheriff of Broken Bow. Tragan had stopped now, and was looking ahead. He was on the left bank of the stream, across from Merritt.

Coolly Merritt slipped a cartridge out of his belt, raised his arm, and tossed the cartridge down into the stream. It splashed into the water about a dozen feet from where Finn Tragan sat his horse.

The sheriff's right hand snaked down to his gun, and the gun slid halfway out of the holster. He held it there, his head swiveling, moving up to the top of the bluff, and then he saw Merritt sitting there, hat pulled low over his eyes, watching.

Tragan stared at him for some time, saying nothing, and then he rode slowly up the slope.

Merritt said to him, "Afternoon, Sheriff."

Tragan nodded. His thin, almost swarthy face showed nothing. His amber-colored eyes were narrowed. He said, "You're Merritt Kane, chap bought the Goodman place."

"That's right," Merritt nodded. He puffed on

his cigarette and said casually, "Looking for someone, Sheriff?"

Tragan blinked, not expecting this abrupt question. He said, "Just ridin', mister."

"Nice country," Merritt nodded, "but pretty rough on a railroad."

"Yeah," Tragan said. He glanced at Merritt sharply, and then he stared down at the line of stakes.

Merritt said evenly, "I could have picked a better route through these hills, if it was my job to make the survey for the line."

Finn Tragan moistened his lips. "You a surveyor, Kane?" he asked.

Merritt shook his head. "I've seen railroads laid out before," he stated. "I don't like the looks of this one."

"Tell it to the railroad," Tragan said sourly, and he turned his horse to go.

As he moved off, Merritt said softly, "I might do that, Sheriff."

Finn Tragan flashed him a quick significant look, but he kept riding down the slope, back in the direction of Broken Bow. Merritt finished his cigarette and tossed it away. He cut across the hills, leaving the line of stakes, and he entered the valley in which the surveyors were camped, coming in from a different direction this time.

The white-topped wagon was still parked in

the same spot. It was nearly dusk now, and the cook fire was going. The surveyors had made no progress beyond the point at which Merritt had seen them on the way in. He wondered if the ranchers of Broken Bow were still posting guards at the mouth of the valley, keeping the surveyors at a distance.

Skirting the wagon at the far side of the valley, and moving soundlessly, Merritt soon found this out. As he came up out of the valley a dark figure stepped out on a rock, rifle in hand.

The man said tersely, "All right, mister. That's far enough."

Merritt stopped. He said, "I'm Merritt Kane— just bought the Goodman place today. I'm on your side."

The sentinel lowered the rifle, took a good look in the gathering dusk, and said, "You sure knocked hell out o' Red Kramer last night, Kane. He had it comin', too."

The voice was vaguely familiar, and Merritt stared at the man. He was in the shadows, and his face could not be seen clearly. Merritt said, "Who are you, mister?"

"Red Kramer," the man chuckled. "Come on up, Kane."

Merritt rode up. He sat on the horse, looking down at Kramer, and he said, "You take it nicely, Red."

"Hell," Kramer grinned, "I had a few too many

over in Milltown before I hit the Wild West. Never had no right to pick on that West kid." He laughed. "Guess it's because I got no use for his damned brother."

Merritt smiled. "Stephen West," he said. "Why not?"

"For one thing," Kramer growled, "he's marryin' Sabine Bell, an' I don't like that. For another thing, West comes in here without a dime, an' in six or seven months he's just about runnin' the town."

Merritt stared at him. "West came here without a dime?" he repeated.

"How I heard it," Kramer said tersely, "Asa Creel's backin' him at the bank. Ben Lowden, who owns Hatchet, heard that. Ben knows people at the bank."

"I see," Merritt murmured.

This was a new bit of information on the amazing career of Stephen West. He thought about that as he rode back to Broken Bow.

It was night when he came into town and stabled his horse at the hotel livery. The southbound stage had just pulled in, and passengers were getting out of the coach in front of the stage office.

There was a small crowd around the stage, indicating that someone of importance was coming to Broken Bow. Merritt slowed down in front of the hotel, and he stood there, watching the passengers getting down. He spotted Stephen

West in the crowd, and Asa Creel, president of the bank.

On the hotel porch he heard a foot scrape, and looking up he saw the hotel clerk, peering down the street, yellow lamplight reflecting on his spectacles. Noticing Merritt, he nodded and said, "It's starting now, Mr. Kane."

"What?" Merritt asked.

"Railroad," the clerk announced in a satisfied manner. "That's Mr. Peter Dunstan getting off the stage."

Merritt noticed that a girl was getting off too, a girl in a gray traveling cape. In the light outside the stage depot he could see the color of her hair—reddish brown. She was very pretty, and she was chatting gaily as she stepped down from the coach. Stephen West had come over to assist her.

"Who is Peter Dunstan?" Merritt asked, still watching the passengers.

"Representative of Great Kansas," the clerk told him. "They're setting up quarters here in Broken Bow. You'll see action now, Mr. Kane."

They were coming toward the hotel, the girl with the reddish hair, walking with West and another man, a tall, gray-haired, distinguished-looking man in eastern clothes. He wore a huge gold watch chain across his fawn-colored vest, and as he walked he had his hand tucked inside the vest pocket.

"Made reservations here," the clerk was saying. "Peter Dunstan and sister, Miss Fay Dunstan, of Chicago."

A hostler from the stage stables was carrying a number of bags, coming up behind them. Merritt stepped aside to let them pass. Stephen West saw him and nodded briefly.

The tall man, Peter Dunstan, glanced his way. He had a long nose like a prow, and a habit of sniffing as he walked. His sister was tall, and in no way resembling him. She was talking gaily with Stephen West as they passed Merritt, but she saw him, and she noticed him, her talk dragging a bit. He could not tell the color of her eyes, but he imagined that they would be light blue to go with that hair. Her voice was soft, modulated, and Merritt Kane was struck with the contrast between Fay Dunstan and Sabine Bell. Fay had been around; she'd met people. Sabine Bell was more like a man. She'd spent her time on the ranch, keeping it going. She probably did not dress up very much. She would not know how to wear clothes the way Fay Dunstan wore them.

The party passed on into the hotel, and Merritt, coming behind them, going up to his room, saw them at the desk. The clerk was fawning over them, making jokes because these people were important.

As he was going up the stairs he saw Fay

Dunstan turn and glance up at him deliberately. He nodded slightly with his head, and he was rewarded with a smile. He was frowning when he reached the top step and went down the corridor to his room. Fay Dunstan was remarkably attractive, the kind of girl a man did not meet too often in a town like Broken Bow. Merritt had met many women in many towns, all the wrong kind of women, and he'd learned to stay away from them. This girl was as different from them as a diamond is from glass.

In his room he cleaned up and shaved, and then went downstairs for supper in the hotel dining room. He was quite sure that Peter Dunstan and his sister would be there, too, and they were. They sat at a corner table. Asa Creel, the banker, and Stephen West were with them.

Taking a table across the room, Merritt had his meal, glancing now and then across the room at the four people there. He heard Fay Dunstan's tinkling laughter every once in a while, and he wondered what Sabine Bell thought of her fiancé's entertaining a girl like this. Sabine would undoubtedly have to understand that Stephen West was going to be a big man in Broken Bow, and that occasionally he would have to be away on affairs like this. Merritt wondered how she would take that.

West saw him after a while as he was lighting up a cigar. The real-estate man turned his head slightly, gave Merritt a searching stare, and then looked the other way.

Merritt got up when he'd finished and went out into the night, turning up in the direction of the Wild West Saloon. It was early in the evening and Big Sam McGee was standing outside, a cigar in his mouth, having just finished the evening meal. He nodded when Merritt came up, and he said, "A little poker tonight?"

"That could be," Merritt smiled. He heard the piano inside, the player just idling along lazily, a chord here and there, light little runs, like a fairy hand on the keys.

Sam McGee said, nodding toward the door, "Born musician. Never heard the like of it, and I been in Europe."

"How'd they get to be brothers?" Merritt asked.

McGee shook his head. "That's how it goes, Kane," he said.

Merritt went inside. He saw Jonathan West at the piano, and the young man turned his head, saw him, and nodded pleasantly. Merritt went over to him, stood there for a few moments, watching West's hands on the keys, and then he said, "How long do you stay in this town, Jonathan? How long do you die?"

Jonathan West shrugged. "There'll be a change someday," he promised, but it was not a strong promise, and Merritt could see that this boy needed a push. He needed someone behind him all the time, or that amazing talent would be wasted. Jonathan said, "Heard you bought the Goodman place, Mr. Kane. Glad you're staying with us."

"I'll be here a while," Merritt murmured.

He drifted away, and after a while he sat down at one of the card tables, joining three other men at their invitation. He played till past eleven o'clock, and then he had had enough. He hadn't lost anything, and he hadn't won anything, and he was satisfied. He'd passed an evening.

As he walked toward the door, Sam McGee lifted a hand to him from his place at the end of the bar. He nodded and went outside. The town was not too crowded tonight. As he walked up the street toward the hotel a cool breeze came down to him from the north end of the draw. It felt good on his face.

This was a quiet evening and a quiet town, the way he had expected it to be when he headed this way many weeks before after turning in his star. This was the way it would always be if the railroad did not build to Broken Bow and stop here.

Groups of men sat around on the porches in front of saloons, their cigars and pipes glowing in the shadows. He could hear their low talk as he went by, and occasional deep-chested laughs.

Passing the white-steepled church, he could hear the choir practicing inside, and it was a nice sound. A baby was crying in one of the buildings as he walked past, and then on the next corner he saw Jonathan West and Roxy Bell leaning against a hitching rack, talking.

As he went by, Jonathan said to him, "A nice evening, Mr. Kane."

Merritt nodded. He glanced at Roxy, but it was too dark here to see her face. She didn't say anything to him, and he went on, wondering what the girl expected him to do about her sister. Sabine had given no indication that she was tiring of Stephen West, and as long as she felt that way about him it did not make sense to try to move in.

He walked down along the street, intending to go straight to the hotel, but on the spur of the moment he left the boardwalk and crossed the road toward a cigar store on the opposite side. He'd noticed the store there earlier in the day.

He was out in the middle of the road, about halfway across, when the shot rang out from the dark alley on the side of the street he'd just left.

Out of the corner of his eye he saw the orange flare of the gun, and he felt the drive of the bullet as it grazed his cartridge belt, spinning him slightly.

Recovering, he dropped to one knee, his gun in hand, firing twice into the alley. Then he got up, face set tightly, and he sprinted straight for the alley, ducking under the hitching rail, firing twice more into the shadows as he went up on the walk.

No return fire came from the alley, indicating that either the man had been hit in that first volley from the road or he'd fired one bullet and fled, taking no chances.

Merritt heard footsteps at the far end of the alley as he plunged into it. He fired one more shot at random, and then he slowed down, backed against the right wall, and reloaded. He went up more slowly, feeling his way, hearing the crowd gather outside.

A man was yelling, "Where's Sheriff Tragan?"

Merritt came out into the open at the far end of the alley, his gun tight in his hand, peering into the shadows. The night was dark, with no moon, and he could see little. He was in a vacant lot here, and the stars were small pin points of light above him. He could hear the breeze rustle the dry weeds, but nothing else. His assailant had fled after taking that single shot at him.

The thought came to him then that he'd been closer to death than he'd at first believed. The killer had been waiting for him in that alley, knowing he would pass that way as he walked back to the hotel. Probably not more than a half-dozen feet would have separated them if he hadn't suddenly crossed the road before coming up to the mouth of the alley. At six feet a man could not miss.

He didn't want to have to answer a lot of foolish questions from the crowd at the head of the alley, so he walked across to the next block, turned down again to the main street, and then walked into the hotel.

In his room he lighted the lamp after first pulling down the blind, and this time as he lighted it he did not put himself between the lamp and the window so that his shadow would be thrown on the shade. Locking the door, he unbuckled his gun belt and sat down on the bed, a grim frown on his face.

In Broken Bow he'd already made an enemy, an enemy who hated or feared him so much that he lay in wait in a dark alley to shoot him down. He was not sure yet why anyone would want him out of the way. No one had been after his money. A footpad would have used a knife or a section of lead pipe on him as he passed the alley. Only a man who wanted him dead would have opened up on him with a gun as he was out in the middle of the road with people in the vicinity.

He looked at the gun belt in his hands, at the smooth-handled Colt and the oily holster, the black leather reflecting the light of the lamp. He hadn't expected to use that gun on anyone, ever, but that was not to be. In Broken Bow someone wanted him dead—not frightened so that he would leave and not bother them, but dead. That bullet had been fired with the intent to kill.

A cold anger swept through him, and he knew now that come hell, high water, or the railroad, he was going to stay and see this through.

CHAPTER SEVEN

AT TEN O'CLOCK the next morning Arch Goodman drove into Broken Bow in a rented buckboard, yanked his bags out at the stage depot, and purchased his ticket for Chicago. He was dressed in his Sunday best and clean-shaven, and he wore a tie.

Coming out of the hotel, Merritt spotted him talking with a group of men outside the station. He went over, and Goodman waved a hand to him.

He said to Merritt, "Place is yours, Kane. Left everything in it just the way you saw it. Just took out my clothes. Good luck."

Merritt shook hands with him. He said, "I'll take a run out this morning." He had to make a list of the things he would need to put the place in order, and he wanted to get a better look at the property he'd purchased so hastily. He was remembering, too, Sabine Bell's offer to show him around, wondering whether he ought to accept it. Stephen West would not be too pleased, but then, West was seeing quite a lot of Fay Dunstan.

"Must be a hundred an' fifty beeves out in the hills," Arch Goodman told him. "Tom Morse will help you look 'em up."

Merritt nodded. The stage was ready to leave. Goodman got on, and as the coach pulled away Merritt went back to the hotel.

Fay Dunstan was standing on the porch, alone, watching him come. She was dressed in white and she carried a pink parasol. Her eyes were blue, a very light blue, the color of the early-morning sky.

Merritt touched his hat. He was about to pass on up to his room when the girl said, "It's an interesting town, is it not?"

Merritt paused at the top step. He caught the odor of lilac perfume, faint and yet distinct. He said, "Reckon I'm new in this town myself, ma'am. I like it."

"You—you're Mr. Merritt Kane," Fay Dunstan smiled. "Mr. West pointed you out to me. You're a rancher in Broken Bow."

"Aim to be," Merritt smiled. "Haven't even taken possession of my place yet." He nodded his head toward the coach rolling down the street. "I bought the property from the old gentleman leaving Broken Bow on that stage."

Miss Dunstan took a step closer to him. She said huskily, "It must be wonderful to be a rancher, to raise cattle on the open range. I've heard so much about it."

Merritt fumbled for his tobacco bag and started to roll a cigarette. He said, "Not so wonderful when you go to look up what's left of your herd after the winter blizzards, and you find bags of bones strewn in the valleys."

He leaned back against the porch pillar, putting the cigarette in his mouth, and as he did so he saw Sabine Bell riding by on her roan horse. She looked up at him, nodded a little coldly, he thought, and kept on down the street. He wondered why she should be cold.

Fay Dunstan said, looking after Sabine, "A very stunning girl." She laughed, the same tinkling laugh Merritt had heard in the restaurant the previous night, and she said archly, "She wouldn't be your lady friend, would she, Mr. Kane?"

Merritt lighted the cigarette and tossed the match into the street. "Not mine," he said. "Stephen West's. They're engaged to be married."

Fay said, "Oh," and he could not be sure whether she was a little annoyed, or just amused. She was still smiling, watching Sabine dismount in front of the Empire Dry Goods Store. She said, "I'd like to see your place someday, Mr. Kane."

"That might be arranged," Merritt murmured, and then Peter Dunstan came through the door.

He nodded to Merritt coldly, and he said, "Are you ready, Fay?"

"Mr. Merritt Kane, Peter," she introduced them. "My brother, Mr. Kane."

Peter Dunstan shook Merritt's hand and let it go. He said, "West tells me you beat him to the purchase of a ranch in this section, Mr. Kane."

Merritt shrugged. "My price was better," he stated, "and I'm buying to stay." He implied that Stephen West had not been buying for that reason.

Dunstan said thoughtfully, "Any man purchasing property in and around Broken Bow these days, Mr. Kane, is a wise man. We expect to have the rails here by early winter." He said this in a rather unnecessarily loud voice, so that the few other men sitting on the porch nearby could hear him.

Merritt was all set to make a remark concerning the route the surveyors had made through the Yellow Hills. It was on the tip of his tongue, but he didn't say it. He wasn't sure, himself, why. He said, "You'll have to move pretty fast to make it before winter sets in."

The Great Kansas man shrugged airily. "We expect to swing this branch down from Ralston, and that's only two hundred and fifty miles away, Mr. Kane. Railroad building is not what it was ten or fifteen years ago. We move fast these days once we start to lay track."

You won't move fast through the Yellow Hills, Merritt was thinking, not after you see the route those blockheads have laid out for you.

Peter Dunstan had taken his sister's arm and they went down the steps, Fay Dunstan nodding to Merritt. She called back, "Nice meeting you, Mr. Kane."

"My pleasure," Merritt said. He walked through the hotel, went to the livery stable in the rear, and saddled the gray. As he rode down the alley and out to the street he saw Jonathan West standing on the walk, watching him.

Young West came over hastily, and he said, "Was that shot fired at you last night, Mr. Kane?"

Merritt nodded. "Reckon it was," he said. "Came out of the alley down the street."

"You went in after him," Jonathan said, "and then we lost track of you."

"I didn't find him," Merritt smiled coldly, "but I will before I'm through in this town."

"You'd better be careful," Jonathan warned. "Who would want to shoot you, Mr. Kane?"

"I'll find that out, too," Merritt said.

He saw Sabine Bell coming out of the dry goods store with a package, mounting her horse, and he rode that way, moving up beside her as she started to leave town. He said, "Good morning, Miss Bell."

Sabine nodded to him. "Going out to your property?"

Merritt stared straight ahead of him. "Figured you might like to show me the range boundaries," he stated. "Nice morning for a ride."

He saw her frown a little, and then she said, "I made a promise. I'll keep it."

"No need to if you're busy," Merritt observed.

"I'm not busy," Sabine said a little testily.

Merritt shrugged, and he was smiling a little. He repeated, "Nice morning for a ride."

Sabine Bell turned to look at him as they left the last house on the street and started up the slope out of the draw. She said tersely, "You try mighty hard, Mr. Kane, to make an impression on a girl."

Merritt pushed his hat back a little. "Not another man's girl," he said gently.

Sabine didn't say anything to that. She rode on rather grimly, and then she said, "Who were the strangers back at the hotel?"

"Peter Dunstan," Merritt told her. "Great Kansas representative."

"And his wife?" Sabine asked.

"His sister," Merritt murmured. He didn't look at the girl at his side.

"She's very pretty," Sabine said. She changed the subject. She said, "What did Mr. Dunstan have to say about the railroad?"

"They expect the rails to reach here by early winter," Merritt told her. "That's the plan."

Sabine laughed coldly. "The surveyors haven't got out of the valley yet," she stated. "We have different men stationed up there every day to stop them. What are your plans concerning the railroad, Mr. Kane?"

Merritt looked down at the gray's head. He said, "If they're coming, they'll come, Miss Bell, unless you want to start a war to stop them."

"We're not starting a war," Sabine said testily.

"If they bring a crew up here to push their way out of the valley," Merritt stated, "what will it be? You can't put a gun in a man's hand, station him somewhere, and then expect him to run away when trouble starts."

"So you'd let the road come through," Sabine said tersely, "without making any attempt to block them."

"If it comes," Merritt said.

Sabine stared at him. "Why do you keep saying 'if'?" she asked. "Everybody knows it's coming. You said yourself that a Great Kansas representative was in town to set up quarters here."

"Plans are made and plans are changed," Merritt said. "I aim to sit tight and wait."

They were coming abreast of Double Bell ranch now, and Merritt wondered whether she'd turn off, but she didn't. She was going on with him to his own place. He felt good about that.

Leaving the Double Bell ranch behind, they moved up into the higher hills, through the clumps of timber, and then Sabine stopped very suddenly. She was staring straight ahead of her, and then Merritt saw it, too. A column of gray-white smoke was lifting up into the air from a point about a mile distant.

"That's a fire," Sabine said quickly. She stared

at him, her eyes wide with concern. "That—that's the Goodman place up there."

Without a word, Merritt touched the spurs to the gray, and the big animal shot forward. He heard Sabine Bell coming behind him as he tore up the slope, ducking under a few overhanging pine branches, coming out into one of the parks. Then he saw the fire below him—a big blaze, his own ranchhouse, clouds of smoke pouring up from the fire.

He stopped because the entire house was aflame, and a hundred men with buckets couldn't stop it now. Sabine came up, pulling to a stop beside him, and they stared at the flames, neither one of them saying anything. The place was deserted. They could hear nothing but the crackle of flames, and then the roar and sizzle as the roof fell in. Showers of sparks poured up into the sky.

Merritt touched the gray and he went down the slope at a slow trot, his face gray, eyes seeming to have receded in his head.

Sabine said to him, "Maybe Goodman was careless with his breakfast fire this morning. Maybe—"

"No," Merritt broke in on her, almost savagely. He was thinking of the money he'd put down on this place, the way he'd earned that money through the years, wearing the five-pointed star, wearing it there on his chest like a target for every bloodthirsty killer's gun in the toughest towns in the West. "That fire was started," Merritt said slowly.

They felt the heat of the burning building and they had to stop again now. He noticed that the little bunkhouse was not burned, and he was thinking that he could make his quarters there until he was able to build again, but building would cost money, a lot of money, and after buying the Goodman property he didn't have too much left.

"How do you know it was started?" Sabine asked curiously.

"Someone took a shot at me from an alley in Broken Bow last night," Merritt told her. "This is another phase of it."

Sabine was silent. Then she said, "Why? You haven't made any real enemies in this town, have you? You had a fight with Kramer of Hatchet, but Red never held a grudge against anyone."

"It wasn't Kramer," Merritt said. He rode on again, this time making a wide circuit of the burning building. He found what he wanted after about ten minutes, and then he came back to where Sabine was waiting for him. He said briefly, "Two riders pulled away from here probably an hour or so ago. Tracks head east. I'm going after them."

Sabine said, "I can send some of our riders with you."

Merritt shook his head. "My fight," he said

quietly. "Thanks anyway." He touched his hat to her and he rode around the still-burning ruin, picking up the tracks on the other side. They were easy to follow, the two riders having made no attempt to conceal their track, and that was not a good sign. They had several opportunities the next few miles to do so, too, but they ignored them. The tracks went down into streams and across shale that left little or no impression, and with the slightest effort they could have confused him by swinging to the north or south at right angles from this eastward trek. They didn't, and in another half hour the tracks went into the stage road leading to Broken Bow. They were lost there in the score of other hoofmarks.

Merritt stared down the road. It was early afternoon now, and if the two men who'd set fire to the Goodman place had kept going, they were in Broken Bow at this moment, and in a town of a thousand persons, locating them would be out of the question.

He entered Broken Bow after two o'clock in the afternoon, with the sun hot and very little air along the main street. He'd been hoping on the way in that he'd spot two horses at the hitching racks along the street—horses that showed evidence of having been ridden fairly hard recently—but he didn't. There were a few horses scattered here and there, swishing their tails at the flies, standing three-legged, but none of them were sweating. He could not even be sure about that. Very possibly the two men had ridden at a leisurely pace into Broken Bow, and their horses by this time would have recovered.

Pulling up in front of the Wild West, he went inside, finding Big Sam McGee sitting at an empty table, an old newspaper spread out before him. A swamper was cleaning out the saloon, moving his brush in and out among the tables.

McGee waved a hand, and Merritt came over and sat down. He said quietly, "You see a lot of things in this town, Sam. See two riders come through here within the last hour or so?"

Big Sam looked at him. "Tearin' past outside?"

Merritt shook his head. "They wouldn't have to be going too fast," he said.

"Two fellers stopped in here for a drink a little past noon," McGee said. "Didn't seem to be in no hurry."

Merritt moistened his lips. "Recognize them?" he asked.

McGee scowled. "Never seen them before," he said. "What's the trouble, Kane?"

"I was burned out this morning," Merritt told him. "I followed two riders away from my place. They could have come this way." Even as he said it he realized there was a good possibility that they'd gone the other way after turning into the stage road. If they had, he would never know.

"Burned you out!" Sam McGee was repeating dumbly. "You ain't even lived in it yet."

"I never will now," Merritt said. He went over to the bar and had a glass of cold beer. He stood there, drinking it, the bitterness riding through him now.

In the bar mirror he saw Finn Tragan coming through the door, and he heard Sam McGee say grimly, "Somebody burned out Kane's place, Sheriff. Property he just bought from Arch Goodman."

Tragan didn't reply to McGee. He came over to the bar and placed both hands on the wood. He said, "That right, Kane?"

"That's right," Merritt said briefly.

"Know who did it?" Tragan asked him.

Merritt turned around slowly, looking full into Tragan's amber-colored eyes. He fancied he saw a faint triumph there, but he could not be sure about that. He said, "If I knew I wouldn't have to tell you about it, mister."

Tragan laughed shortly, and it was not a pleasant laugh. He said, "Get the law behind you, Kane. You're on the safe side then."

"Am I?" Merritt asked.

Finn Tragan ordered a beer. He said, "See any sign of 'em, Kane?"

"No," Merritt said. He paid for his drink.

"Maybe it was an accident," Tragan grinned. "Maybe Goodman left the fire—"

"It wasn't," Merritt said coldly. He stepped away from the bar, nodded to Sam McGee, and went outside. He stood on the porch for a moment, looking up and down the street, and he discovered that he was very hungry now. Following that trail, he'd forgotten about food, but now that there was nothing else that he could do, he was hungry.

He went over to the hotel, passed through the lobby, and entered the dining room. He met the Dunstans and Stephen West just coming out.

West stopped. He was smiling blandly. He said, "Been looking over your property, Mr. Kane? I saw you ride out this morning."

"I looked it over," Merritt nodded. He glanced at Fay Dunstan, who was smiling at him.

"Worth the money you paid for it?" West asked, and there was a peculiar note in his voice.

Merritt looked at him, his pulse beginning to pound. He said, "I was burned out this morning, Mr. West."

Fay Dunstan let out a little cry of concern, and Stephen West's eyes widened.

"Burned out?" West repeated. His pale eyes were hooded now, but concern was on his face, in the tone of his voice.

"That's right," Merritt said. "I was burned out." He gave them no more information. Pushing past them, he sat down at a corner table, and the thought was pounding at him relentlessly: He knew. He knew!

Chapter Eight

EARLY THAT AFTERNOON he rode out of Broken Bow with Tom Morse, and the lank man said disconsolately, "Gets me, Kane. That place has been standin' there for thirty years, an' nobody in this town ever liked that old crab Arch Goodman. The day *he* goes, *you're* burned out. Why?"

"I don't know," Merritt said. "I want to get our stock rounded up and I want to keep an eye on them. They might go after the stock next."

"Why?" Tom Morse asked and spat into the road.

"I don't know," Merritt said again.

"Hell," Morse said shrewdly, "ain't nobody runnin' down nobody else without a reason, Kane."

"I'll find that reason," Merritt promised him.

As they rode past the Double Bell ranch, Sabine Bell came up the slope toward him, and Merritt had the feeling that she'd been watching, expecting him to come out again.

She said when she came up, "Find anything, Mr. Kane?"

"They went into Broken Bow," Merritt said briefly. "I lost them."

"I sent a couple of our riders over to round up

your stock," Sabine told him. "I thought you'd be coming out to do that."

Merritt looked at her. "Thanks," he said. "We're going out now." He found a quiet little pleasure in her thoughtfulness.

"You can run your stock over this way," Sabine offered, "and bunk with us if you want. Plenty of room with the boys."

"We'll make out," Merritt told her. "Much obliged." He was thinking of Stephen West again, the man who was going to marry this girl, and he suddenly did not like that a bit.

They rode on, and they located their herd, three Double Bell riders with them. The 150-odd head of cattle had been rounded up during the afternoon, and were now held in a little park about a quarter of a mile from the burned ranch house.

One of the Double Bell men said to Merritt, when he came up, "Tough, Kane."

"I'll make it up," Merritt told him. "Thanks for the help."

He sat there with Tom Morse when the riders moved off through the timber, and he said softly, "That's all we have, Tom. I don't want to lose them."

"You will," Morse growled. "Why be proud, Kane? Move this bunch in with Sabine Bell's herd an' they won't touch you."

Merritt shook his head. "I don't like to do

business like that," he said briefly. "I'm not hiding behind a woman."

Morse shrugged. "If they tried to shoot you down in Broken Bow last night, an' they burned you out this morning, stands to reason they'll come after your stock next."

"Reckon they will," Merritt nodded.

"You have to sleep sometime," Morse observed, "an' there's only two of us. No tellin' how many there are of them."

Merritt looked at him. "You want to ride back to town, Morse?" he asked.

The lank man reddened. He said stiffly, "Kane, Runnin' G is my brand. If you figure on stayin', I do, too."

Merritt smiled a little. He said, "Thanks, Tom." He wondered again at the love and respect a man had for a brand, for a sign on the flank of a steer or a cow. Morse had never particularly liked Arch Goodman. He'd called the old man a crab. But Running G was the brand Tom Morse worked for, and he still intended to stay on blindly, even though he knew there was liable to be trouble.

"Reckon we kin take turns sleepin'," Morse said. "We kin push the stock up closer to the bunkhouse. I don't need much sleep, Kane."

At the burned-out Running G ranch they put the old bunkhouse in order, cleaned it out a bit, stowed away their gear, and then rounded up

Arch Goodman's stock, driving the animals up closer to the ranch.

It was hot work, moving in and out of the timber, chasing small bands of cattle ahead of them. The stock was in good condition, an indication that Arch Goodman's range was excellent grazing ground.

"Old fool," Tom Morse growled once. "He could o' made money out here if he'd bought more stock an' expanded. Arch was set in his ways. He started out as a small rancher. He aimed to be a small rancher when he died. Damned if I know why. That was Arch."

In late afternoon as they were bringing in the last strays, Merritt noticed that it had grown cooler. A haze had started to come up in front of the sun, and Morse frowned and said, "Rain before midnight, Merritt, or I'm a ring-tailed monkey. Nice weather for cattle rustlers or anybody else likes to go prowlin' around after dark."

Merritt didn't like it either. He knew beyond any shadow of doubt that the same ones who had burned him out would go after his stock next, and tonight, with the rain coming, would be an ideal time.

Back at the bunkhouse they ate in silence, and as Merritt came outside to wash up, he felt the first drops of rain on his face. Heavy clouds were drifting across the mountains to the west, and they heard the distant rumble of thunder.

Tom Morse said laconically, "Even if rustlers don't grab 'em, this thunderstorm will spook 'em so's they'll scatter from here to kingdom come."

Merritt went to the shed behind the bunkhouse, and when he came back it was already raining hard. He unfolded his slicker, hung it on a hook near the door, and said, "I'll turn in now, Tom. Wake me at midnight."

"You'll take the tough watch," Morse stated. "That it?"

"My cattle," Merritt told him.

He sat down on the bunk, kicked off his boots, and in five minutes was asleep. He could hear the rain on the roof and the rumble of thunder, coming closer all the time.

He awoke with the lamplight shining in his face. Morse had come in, water streaming from his slicker, and he'd lit the lamp. It was still raining, but there was no more thunder. It was a steady downpour now, and Morse said sourly, "Rainin' like hell, Merritt. Anybody comes out in this weather can have that stock."

"See anything?" Merritt asked him.

"Can't see a hand in front o' your face," Morse told him. "Stock didn't spook, though. Thunder an' lightnin' didn't git as bad as I've seen it."

They had a cup of coffee, and then Merritt put on the slicker, went out to the shed, and saddled the gray. It was still raining hard, but it seemed to be letting up a little. He pulled his hat low over his face, turned up the collar of the slicker, and rode through the trees to the open meadow where they'd brought the stock that afternoon.

He couldn't see them clearly, but he could hear them occasionally moving in the darkness. He sat astride the gray under the dripping trees at the edge of the meadow.

After a while the rain stopped, but it still dripped from the trees, and he moved his position out into the open. He was deliberating whether he should risk a smoke when he heard the sudden shout, and then the three quick shots from the north end of the meadow.

Other shots came from the west side, and then the cattle were up and moving. Merritt pushed the gray into action. He could make out the dim figure of a rider coming up behind the bunched stock, yelling, firing his gun.

His own gun in hand, Merritt drove the gray toward this man. They were pushing the stock toward the south, pushing them hard. Another rider came into view, and then a third. Merritt could not tell if there were more. He was within thirty yards of them now, lifting his gun, when the gray stepped into a hole.

The big animal went down hard, Merritt kicking himself clear. He hit soft earth, but as he rolled his head came into contact with a stone jutting out of the ground. Light exploded through his head. He got up on his knees, stumbled forward, and fell again, hearing the shouts and the running of the stock ahead of him. He was sick and weak, and consciousness left him.

Tom Morse found him fifteen minutes later, the gray horse having stopped and come back. Morse saw the horse and found the rider on the ground. Merritt was coming out of it by this time. He sat on the muddy ground, shaking his head, and Morse said, "That gray go down?"

Merritt stood up, a little shaky yet. He said, "They were headed south. We shouldn't have too much trouble following them."

"Tonight?" Morse asked him.

"Tonight," Merritt said grimly. He rubbed the side of his head gingerly as he stepped into the saddle again.

"How many were there?" Morse asked. "Heard them shots an' I come arunnin'."

"I saw three," Merritt told him. "There may have been more."

"Three is plenty," Morse murmured.

They had no trouble following the trail even in the darkness. They knew the general direction in which the stock had been run, and the 150 head had left a wide path. Occasionally Merritt dismounted, struck a match, and held it close to the ground to make sure that they hadn't left the trail. The churned hoofprints were in the mud.

Merritt said, "Know this country, Tom?"

"Some," Morse nodded. "Ain't much down

this way. You go far enough an' you run into the Catamount Range—low mountains, pretty good territory for rustlers. Used to be a bunch of 'em hidin' in there, but the Cattlemen's Association drove 'em out. That was years ago."

"How far to this range?" Merritt wanted to know.

"Keep pushin'," Morse told him, "an' we'll be there in the mornin'."

The moon came out after a while, making it still more simple to follow the trail of the rustled stock. They made good time, and an hour before dawn they were moving up into the low hills, the foothills of the Catamount Range. They hit timber again here, having left it some distance behind, and they held up for fifteen minutes, giving the horses a chance to blow. They made cigarettes and they squatted down on their heels to smoke them.

Morse said, "Pretty soon."

Merritt took out his Colt gun, examined the charges, and then slipped it back into the holster. They were moving again, climbing higher into the hills, dipping down into narrow valleys.

Then Tom Morse said, "Place up ahead here another mile or so, I remember. Used to be a hangout here for a band o' hoss thieves. They had a corral an' a shack. We hung up two of 'em out in front o' the shack, an' there's nobody been livin' out here since."

"Anybody knows this country," Merritt said, "might head for that hideout. That how you figure it?"

"Every loose rider in this territory knows about the hideout," Morse nodded. "If this bunch that's after your hide paid a couple o' boys to run off your stock, they'd know damn well where to go with 'em."

"We'll go in easy," Merritt said.

There was already light in the sky now, coming in very slowly. They could see quite a distance ahead of them as they rode, and the trail of the herd they were following was very clear on the ground. The riders had bunched them as they pushed south toward the Catamount Range.

"Over that next rise," Morse said. "You kin see the place from the top. This trail leads straight there. Reckon if they ain't stoppin' there for good, they'll pull up for breakfast anyway."

"We'll swing over to the east," Merritt said, "and go in that way. They might have somebody up on the ridge watching their back trail."

They moved away from the trail, dipping into timber again, making their way slowly through the trees, coming up on the valley hideout from the east.

It was quite light now, although the sun still wasn't up. As they came out at the edge of the timber they could look down into a small valley ahead of them.

Tom Morse said succinctly, "There they are, Merritt, all safe an' sound."

Their herd was down below, grazing peacefully along the slopes of the valley. There was an old shack and a broken-down corral at the far end of the valley, and in front of the shack a campfire was going. Three men stood around it, sipping coffee.

"Only three," Morse murmured. "That ain't bad at all."

At the distance of about four hundred yards they could not recognize any of the men. The timber petered out here, too, and it was impossible to approach the valley without being spotted immediately by the men below.

"Kind o' long even for a rifle shot," Morse observed. "What do you think, Merritt?"

"You hole up here," Merritt said. "Get your Winchester out. Give me fifteen minutes to come up behind that shack at the other end of the valley, and then open up on them."

Morse nodded. "Kind o' give 'em a scare," he grinned. "Reckon they ain't figurin' we're this close behind."

"They'll know pretty soon," Merritt grated. He rode off through the timber again, moving along the east rim of the valley. He saw Morse dismount and move up to the edge of the valley, his rifle in hand.

He kept well back from the edge of the valley

himself, taking his time now, knowing that the three men below him were not aware of their presence. He went past the shack, coming up at a point on the rim of the valley just below it. He waited in the timber here, unable to see the men below because they were at the front of the shack.

The sun was moving up now, bringing light to the valley. He could see the smoke of their campfire lifting up into the sky. Their horses were tied close by.

Then Tom Morse's gun started to talk. Merritt saw the puff of white smoke from the east side of the valley, and he heard the yell of alarm from one of the men at the fire.

Morse fired again and again, spacing his shots, and the men raced around the corner of the shack to get out of range of the bullets. Two of them came around to the side where Merritt could see them. The third man either had gone into the shack or was at the other side.

Touching his spurs to the gray, Merritt went down the slope at a gallop, gun in hand, riding straight for the shack. He heard Tom Morse's whoop, and then the two men on his side spotted him. He was still about a hundred yards away, but one of them opened up with his short arm, firing twice, before the two of them made a break for their horses.

Merritt shot at them as they mounted and

spurred away, and he was surprised to see that there were only two of them running. He discovered the reason for that a moment later as he whirled around the corner of the shack. The third man was down on the ground, on his face, arms outstretched. One of Morse's rifle bullets had reached him.

Morse was coming down the valley wall, trying to cut off the two fleeing rustlers, but they were moving pretty fast, heading out the north end of the valley, through which they'd brought the stock. Their horses, too, having had a short rest in the valley, were in much better condition than either Merritt's or Morse's.

Merritt held up his hand, indicating to Morse that it was no use.

The tall rider turned around and trotted toward him. He said when he came up, "Didn't figure that rifle would touch any of 'em, Merritt. That one chap seemed to run right into the lead."

They went back to the shack, dismounted, and walked over to the man on the ground. He had not moved from his position, and Merritt saw the dark stain on the ground below his chest.

"Reckon he's hit pretty bad," Morse observed.

"He's dead," Merritt said, a little disappointed. He'd rolled the man over to look at him. He was a thin-faced, tawny-haired man with a mole on his right cheek. "Know him?" Merritt asked.

Tom Morse nodded. "Saw him around," he

admitted. "Once over in Milltown. He's a loose rider. Lot o' people around here figure he's been runnin' off an occasional head, but nothin' to attract attention. He tried to pull a big job this time. Goes by the name o' Jack Burleigh."

Merritt shook his head. "I'd like to know who sent him," he said quietly. "He didn't pull this job of his own accord. If he'd wanted to rustle stock he'd have picked on Double Bell or one of the big outfits where they might not miss a dozen head or so."

Morse nodded. "So somebody sent this hombre," he said. "Who?"

Merritt scowled. "Let's get this stock back," he said.

"That's what we come for," Tom Morse grinned.

They rode up the slope, pushing the stock ahead of them, moving north out of the valley.

CHAPTER NINE

THEY HAD THE stock back in the meadow near the Running G bunkhouse by eleven o'clock, and Tom Morse, who'd had very little sleep the previous night, turned in.

Merritt hitched up an old buckboard he'd found behind the horse shed, put the gray in the harness, and rode in to Broken Bow for supplies. He'd made a list of the things he would need.

Morse said, "Reckon they won't bother us in the daytime, Merritt."

Riding down the main street an hour later, Merritt saw the workmen fixing up a store next to Stephen West's realty office. Peter Dunstan was outside directing the work, and it was evident that the building would be the temporary quarters of Great Kansas in Broken Bow. West was with Dunstan.

Neither West nor Dunstan saw him, and Merritt drove past, thankful in particular that West hadn't seen him. He didn't want West to know that he could not even buy a horse to pull his buckboard, and had to put his own riding mount in the traces.

He got his order of flour and sugar, coffee, salt pork, bacon, condensed milk, dried apples, and a half-dozen other items he'd listed, and then after hauling the packages out to the buckboard, he crossed over to the Wild West, having seen Big Sam McGee sitting in a chair on the porch outside.

The big man nodded to him as he came up. He said, "Stockin' up, Kane?"

Merritt nodded. He sat down on the top step and looked across the street at Finn Tragan, who had just come out of the restaurant there, and was standing outside the door, picking his teeth.

Merritt said, "What's new in Broken Bow, Sam?"

"Stephen West's sellin' now," McGee told him. "Sold two parcels along Main Street; another one on Fremonte. Gambler from Abilene bought the biggest piece o' ground. Figures on puttin' up a two-story gamblin' hell."

"What about the others?" Merritt asked.

"Two town people," Sam McGee told him. "Mrs. Buckley, the widow owns the dress shop down the street, bought the plot on Fremonte. Figures on puttin' up a larger store when the business boom comes."

Merritt looked at his fingers. He said softly, "I'd say West got quite a bit for the property he bought for a song a while back."

"Quite a bit," McGee told him calmly, "ain't the words, my friend. The Abilene gambler had to lay down a thousand dollars a foot on Main Street."

"Thousand a foot!" Merritt gasped.

McGee nodded. "When the rails get here, Merritt," he stated, "an' the crowds come, that chap will make his money in two months. He knows that. So he pays."

"A thousand dollars a foot," Merritt repeated. "That's big business."

McGee grinned. "You didn't figure Stephen West was a piker, did you, Kane?"

"How much would you say West owns along Main Street?" Merritt asked the bouncer.

"Hard to say," McGee shook his head, "but plenty. Him an' Asa Creel."

"Asa Creel?" Merritt murmured.

"Big banker in town," McGee nodded. "He's bought up quite a few parcels, too. Land around here is harder to get your hands on than hen's teeth, Kane."

"At that price," Merritt smiled, "it would be."

"People know they got to get on the bandwagon now," McGee stated. "With that Dunstan chap here, the Great Kansas means business. Gradin' crews should be along soon."

Merritt watched Finn Tragan ambling easily down the walk, and then he saw the sheriff come to a stop before his buckboard. Tragan had recognized the horse in the traces. Then looking around he spotted Merritt, and he pulled up directly in front of the buckboard. He was standing there, picking his teeth, when Merritt crossed over to the wagon, and for the tenth time Merritt tried to remember where he'd met the man.

Tragan said, "Find them chaps burned you out, Kane?"

"Not yet," Merritt told him. "I will." Again he had the feeling that Tragan was laughing at him inwardly, and he wanted to duck under the hitching rail and hit him in the face.

"Arch must o' left a burnin' cigar around," Tragan said, "just before he pulled out."

Merritt didn't say anything. He untied the gray, stepped up to the seat, and turned the wagon around.

Tragan watched him go, still picking his teeth. He called softly, "Nice-lookin' animal you got in the harness, Kane. Want to sell him?"

Merritt held the gray for one instant, his face turning pale with anger, knowing why Tragan had made the remark. The sheriff of Broken Bow knew he was at the end of his resources financially and he was goading him with this knowledge now.

Merritt said slowly, distinctly, "You own property on Main Street, too, Tragan?"

The question caught Finn Tragan by complete surprise, and his face showed it before he could recover. He reddened, and then his body stiffened a little. He didn't say anything, and Merritt drove off with his supplies.

Fay Dunstan waved a hand to him from the hotel porch, and Merritt nodded back. He would have liked to stop and chat for a few minutes, but he didn't want to leave Tom Morse alone too long.

At the edge of town he passed the telegraph office, and he could hear the instrument clacking away inside. It wasn't until he was out of the draw, approaching the Double Bell ranch, that the thought came to him that he could very easily settle all the doubts in his mind. That telegraph office was the means. He wondered that he hadn't thought about that before, but the whole affair had seemed too preposterous.

He didn't want to turn back now with the rickety buckboard, and he told himself that he would take a ride back later on in the day, send off his wire, and probably get a reply by the following day. He would know then; he would have the answer to a lot of things.

He didn't stop at Double Bell, but pushed on directly to his own place, and was very pleased when he came out into the clearing and saw Sabine Bell and her sister talking with Tom Morse out in front of the bunkhouse. They'd ridden over, and their mounts were tied behind the bunkhouse.

As he came down the dirt road with the buckboard the girls turned to watch him. Sabine said as Merritt stepped down from the seat, "We dropped in to see how you were making out. Tom told us about last night."

"We're still here," Merritt smiled. "Thanks for coming." He added, "Didn't lose a single head last night, either."

"Stocking in supplies?" Sabine asked him. "I guess that means you're staying."

"When I buy a place," Merritt observed, "I stay on it."

"It'll need plenty of fixing," Sabine said. "If you need a few men here to help you when you work on the ranchhouse, let me know. We always have some boys who aren't too busy in the middle of the summer."

"I'll remember it," Merritt nodded.

Roxy Bell looked inside the door of the bunkhouse. She said, "The first thing this place needs is a little cleaning. Don't you have a broom out here, Tom?"

"Cleanin'!" the lank rider grimaced. "Clean it, Miss Bell, an' the next thing you know it's dirty again. Ain't no sense to it."

Roxy grinned at him. She said, "You'd make a poor housewife, Tom."

"I would that," Morse vowed.

The girls left after a while, and Merritt unloaded the buckboard. They worked on the bunkhouse during the late afternoon, repairing the roof, putting it shipshape, and they kept their horses saddled close at hand, ready to ride out.

128

They could see the cattle grazing up on the slope a quarter mile distant. Nothing happened during the afternoon.

When Tom Morse started to think about supper, Merritt said, "I want to get off a wire, Tom. I'll eat in town and get back early before we start the night watches."

"Go ahead," Morse nodded. "Gonna try to raise some more money, Merritt?"

"No," Merritt said slowly. "I want to see where a lot of it is going around here."

He left the ranch and was moving up through the timber when a rider came toward him from the direction of Broken Bow, riding pretty fast. Merritt pulled up, waiting, and then in the gathering dusk he recognized Red Kramer, the Hatchet rider.

Kramer said, "Headin' for Broken Bow, Kane?"

"That's right," Merritt nodded. "What's up, Red?"

"Sam McGee asked me to stop in here on the way past," Kramer told him. "Says he wants to see you right away. Somethin' important."

"Anything wrong?" Merritt asked.

"Not that I could see," Kramer said. "Just that he wants to see you."

Merritt nodded his thanks and turned away. He let the gray horse run as they came into the stage road, and they made very good time. In another fifteen minutes he was at the top of the draw, looking down into Broken Bow. There were clouds in the sky tonight and no moon. He could see Main Street only as a straggling line of yellow lights on both sides of the road.

Moving past the telegraph office, he could see the operator inside, sitting behind his sending instrument, the phones strapped to his head. He'd intended to get his message off first of all, but McGee had something to tell him and the message could wait until he rode out again.

The Wild West was crowded tonight. A long line of horses stood at the hitching rack, and more riders were coming in all the time. He remembered then that it was Saturday night, and on Saturday night the range riders from fifty miles around came in to Broken Bow to howl.

There was a thick cloud of tobacco smoke in the saloon as Merritt came through the doors, and it was still early evening. By midnight he knew he could cut that smoke with a knife.

The card tables were nearly all filled, and there was a crowd around the keno layout. He spotted Sam McGee at the end of the bar, eating a sandwich, big shoulders hunched. McGee had been watching the doors, and when Merritt came in, he nodded to him.

Pushing his way through the crowd, Merritt edged up next to the man. The big bouncer finished his sandwich and wiped his mouth with his handkerchief. He said, "You still lookin' for them chaps burned you out, Merritt?"

Merritt stared at him. "That's right," he said.

Sam McGee nodded. "Remember them two came in here for a drink the afternoon you was followin' somebody from your burned-out place?"

"I remember," Merritt said.

"Didn't recognize them chaps," McGee said. "Strangers in town. They're back again, though."

Merritt moistened his lips, and his gray eyes took on an odd color. He said, "Where?"

"Don't look now," McGee warned. "They're sittin at the card table nearest to the door, one on the right o' the door. Both of 'em facin' us—pock-marked chap, an' the other one has a black beard."

Merritt looked down at the bar. The description McGee had given of the two men was vaguely familiar. He turned slightly, resting one elbow on the wood, and then he glanced casually toward the door, at the same time taking in the card table to the right of the door. Five men were at the table. The two men facing him had their backs to the wall and were studying their cards intently. They had not seen him. He had seen them before. They were the two assistants to the surveyor he'd seen in the valley that first day he'd come to Broken Bow.

The man to his right was pock-marked, a thin,

131

shriveled fellow with furtive, yellowish eyes. The other man had a black beard. He was short and stumpy, with bleary blue eyes.

Merritt said to Sam McGee, "Sure of them, Sam?"

"Never mistake a face," McGee told him positively. "Them chaps came in when this place was empty, too. Had a good look at 'em."

Merritt didn't say anything, realizing that he could be wrong about these two men. He knew only that two men had fired his place, and these two men had ridden into Broken Bow at about the time the two men he'd been following would have reached the town. They could have come from the other direction, from the direction of the valley in which they'd been surveying.

"Much obliged, Sam," Merritt murmured.

"Thought you'd like to know," Sam McGee said. "I'll be around if it gets rough."

Merritt turned to the bartender to order a drink, and as he did so he looked straight into Finn Tragan's face at the far end of the bar. Tragan was leaning over the wood, talking with another man, and he was occupying the identical position McGee usually had at the other end of the bar. Tragan had been watching them.

Chapter Ten

A HALF HOUR AFTER Merritt had come into the Wild West Saloon one of the men at the card table by the door got up to cash in his chips.

Sam McGee said huskily, "All right, Merritt."

Pushing through the crowd, Merritt came up behind the empty chair. He said when some of the men noticed him, "Mind if I sit in, gentlemen?"

The two surveyor's assistants recognized him immediately. The pock-marked man pushed back his chair, the sweat breaking out on his face. He acted for a moment as if he would get up and drop out of the game, and then he relaxed again, evidently deciding that this action would seem suspicious.

The black-bearded man looked steadily at his cards after that first glance at Merritt. His face was expressionless, but his bleary eyes were slightly narrowed.

"Sit down," the man at Merritt's right said carelessly.

Merritt bought some chips from a waiter passing by. He played through two hands, none of the players saying anything, and then after losing a small pot on which he'd raised one of the players, Merritt leaned back in the chair, his body completely relaxed. He rolled a cigarette as one of the players shuffled the cards, and then he started to sniff the air curiously. The pock-marked man, sitting directly opposite him, stared and rubbed his chin.

Merritt said casually, "I smell smoke. Somebody been around a fire lately?"

The pock-marked man's face went the color of dirty clay. He'd been holding a few blue chips in his fingers, and they slipped to the table now. Fear came into his yellow eyes, the kind of expression Merritt had seen in the eyes of mongrel dogs about to be beaten. He wanted to slink away, but he didn't know how to do it.

There was no doubt in Merritt's mind now that these two had fired his place. The black-bearded man sat motionless at the table, staring at the cards as they slid in front of him.

One of the other players, a rider from the Hatchet ranch, said, "I don't smell no smoke, Kane."

"Maybe it's not smoke," Merritt told him softly. "Maybe it's skunk." He looked straight at the pock-marked man, and he was thinking, Who sent you? That's what I want to know. Who sent you?

An uncomfortable silence settled over the table as they continued to play. Merritt saw Stephen West come in, and West glanced his way before going over to the bar to chat with a man there. Finn Tragan was no longer at the far end of the bar. Sam McGee was remonstrating with a half-drunk puncher, a boy of about seventeen. The Wild West was jam-packed now, every card table occupied, no space at the bar, and the crowds still coming in.

Peter Dunstan, the Great Kansas man, came in with Asa Creel, the banker, and they joined West at the bar. Then the black-bearded man at the table with Merritt got up suddenly, saying gruffly, "I'm out." He lurched toward the bar with his chips, cashed them, and went out into the night.

The movement seemed to take the pock-marked man by surprise. He did not like being left alone, and his face showed it. He was pushing his chair back, gathering up his chips, when Merritt's voice reached out at him.

"What's the hurry, friend?"

"Ain't no hurry," the pock-marked man gulped. "No hurry at all, mister."

Merritt sniffed the air as if smelling smoke again, and the pock-marked man looked a little sick. He played through two more hands, and then he got up. He was trembling now, his face covered with a cold sweat. He'd lost heavily on the last two pots, doing this deliberately, Merritt knew, so that he'd have an excuse for dropping out. His chips were gone, and he said a little hoarsely, "I'm cleaned, friends."

He got up, and Merritt got up too, no expression on his face. The pock-marked man swallowed, pushed his chair back, and started for the door. Merritt moved with him, catching the batwing doors as they swung back at him, the pock-marked man going through.

The man paused at the top step of the porch, seeing Merritt come out behind him.

Merritt said, "What's the rush?"

"Ridin' out tonight," the man said doggedly. "What are you followin' me for, mister?"

"Where's your horse?" Merritt asked him.

"Livery in the back," the man muttered.

"Go on back," Merritt told him. "I'm right behind you." He had his hand on his gun now, and the pock-marked man saw that. He started to sweat afresh.

"I ain't done nothin'," he whined.

"Go ahead," Merritt said.

They walked to the head of the alley a short distance from the saloon. The alley was dark, but Merritt could see the patch of light outside the stable entrance. He stayed about five feet behind the man as they went up the alley.

Outside the door of the stable the man stopped, and Merritt pushed him hard through the door, so hard that he staggered. He came up behind the pock-marked man, feeling inside his coat, sliding a Colt gun from his belt.

The stable was empty. A lantern hung from a hook in the ceiling about a dozen feet from them. About half the stalls were occupied, and Merritt could hear the stamping of hoofs. It was a long, low shed, running at right angles to the saloon. The far end was quite dark. A half-dozen bales of hay were strewn near the door, and a pitchfork lay on the top of one of them.

"What do you want from me, mister?" the pock-marked man blubbered.

Merritt tossed the man's gun out through the door behind him. He stepped forward slowly and he said, "Who sent you to fire my place?"

"What place?" the man mumbled.

Merritt hit him in the mouth with his right fist, knocking him back against one of the empty stalls. The blood started to trickle down the man's chin, and the fear was a living thing in his eyes.

"Who sent you?" Merritt asked tersely. "I've been shot at from a dark alley, and I've had my house burned down. I aim to find out who's behind it."

The pock-marked man had no time to reply. The lantern to Merritt's left was suddenly smashed, plunging the stable into darkness. With the breaking of the glass, Merritt automatically dropped to his knees, snaking his gun from the holster.

From the direction of the broken lantern a gun boomed, rocking the stable, an orange flame in the darkness. The slug sang over Merritt's head, passing at about the point where his belt had been. He could hear the rush of boots on the stable floor, and he fired into the darkness.

A man stumbled over him, hammering at his head with the barrel of his gun. They went down on the floor together, rolling over, Merritt slamming his fist into the man's face. There had been two of them making that rush. He was positive of that. Then the pock-marked man joined the melee. They were swinging savagely, and Merritt kept low, punching at them with both fists. He'd lost the gun when the barrel of another gun slashed across his fingers, numbing them.

In the darkness it was impossible to look for the weapon again. He lunged this way and that, driving hard punches at the shadowy figures around him. Once he hit a man full in the face and heard his short scream as he staggered away in the direction of the stable door.

"Get out," a man hissed. "Back door."

He heard them moving away, running in the darkness toward the other end of the stable, and he lunged that way himself. Those bales of hay had been piled along the wall here, and he miscalculated their exact location, his right knee driving into one of them as he ran.

Lurching off balance, he went down, his body rolling against one of the stalls. The horses in the stalls were jumping, whinnying excitedly. Something struck Merritt's head a savage blow as he struggled to his knees, and he rolled away, dazed, sick, coming to a stop on his stomach.

Reaching up to his head, he felt his hair getting sticky with blood, and then a heavier darkness than the darkness in the stable enveloped him.

He thought he heard a man shouting, "Kane—Kane—Merritt Kane!"

Someone was sponging cold water on his face, washing his head with it, the water flowing down into his shirt. He opened his eyes, and the light from the lantern overhead blinded him for a moment. The lantern hung from a hook in the ceiling of the stable.

Big Sam McGee was bent over him, a pail of cold water beside him and a rag in his hand. He was washing the blood from his face, and he said, "All right now? All right now, Merritt?"

Pain exploded through Merritt's head, and he nearly went out again. He fought it off, slowly, grimly, and when he felt better, McGee held a bottle up to his lips.

The bouncer said, "Try some of this."

Merritt drank, and some measure of strength came back to him. He said, "What hit me?"

"Damned sorrel horse, I'd say," McGee stated, nodding toward a sorrel in the nearest stall. "You must o' backed right into him."

"I fell," Merritt frowned. "I'd been chasing them toward that back door."

"Who?" McGee wanted to know. "I heard the shootin' an' I came out on the run. Nobody around when I got to you."

Merritt sat up, feeling his head gingerly. The bleeding had stopped, but he had a nasty cut on the side of his skull. He said to McGee, "Those two burned me out, Sam. I had one of them in here when they put out the light and came at me. There were three of them altogether."

"They had you set up," McGee said solicitously. "You walked right into it, Merritt. We better stop in an' see Doc Barker now, an' have him patch you up a little."

Merritt got to his feet and stood there for a few moments. They located his gun on the floor near the stable entrance, and he put it back into the holster.

Barker's office was a few doors down the street, and the little doctor, making sounds in his throat, cleaned the wound, bandaged it, and sent Merritt off.

"Kicked by a horse," Sam McGee stated.

"That's nice," Barker said dryly. He didn't believe it. Smelling the liquor on Merritt, he'd assumed there had been a brawl and Merritt had been slugged, probably with a gun barrel.

Outside, Merritt said, "I have to get back to Tom Morse. They might make another try at my stock tonight."

"Three of 'em in that stable," McGee mused. "We know who two of 'em were. What about the third chap?"

"He's the one I want," Merritt said tersely.

He didn't go back into the Wild West. His head was still throbbing, and he wanted no more of those tobacco fumes. Getting into the saddle, he went down Main Street, riding slowly, and then as he drew abreast of the telegraph office, he remembered.

Dismounting in front of the office, he went inside. The little room was empty, and the young telegraph operator was busy checking off messages just received. He nodded when Merritt came in.

Merritt picked up the pad and wrote out his message with a stubby pencil on the counter. Then he shoved the pad over to the operator and he said, "How much?"

The young fellow read the message and then looked up at Merritt curiously, a grin breaking out on his face. He said, "This a joke, Mr. Kane?"

"No joke," Merritt frowned. "Get it out tonight."

He paid for the wire and went out. The ride back to the Running G ranch seemed about ten times longer than it usually was. Several times he started to reel in the saddle, but he recovered himself and kept going, moving past Double Bell, up the grades, and then through the timber.

Tom Morse was standing in the bunkhouse door, but the lights were out inside. When he saw Merritt stagger from the horse he came over hurriedly and said, "You kicked by a horse, Merritt?"

Merritt's laugh was low, dry, bitter. "You guessed it, Tom," he said. "Make me a cup of coffee."

They went into the bunkhouse, and the lank rider lit the lamp. He looked at the bandage on Merritt's head and the bruises on his face. He said softly, "Reckon you did run into somethin', Merritt. Maybe a sawmill."

Merritt told him briefly of the encounter in the stable behind the Wild West Saloon, and when he'd finished Morse said, "With that head you better turn in an' let me stand watch tonight."

"Wake me in four hours," Merritt scowled. "I'll be feeling better then." He headed for the bunk, crawled in, after kicking off his boots, and lay there like a dead man, sleep coming to him immediately.

Before falling off, though, he heard Morse moving away from the bunkhouse, whistling softly. He did not sleep soundly. It was a night of feverish tossings, of nightmares. Twice he sat up on the bunk, his body bathed in cold sweat, breathing heavily, the pain in his head.

The third time he awakened he'd been sleeping soundly, and it was not a nightmare that awakened him. It was something else. He lay under the blankets, staring up into the darkness. The door did not close tightly, and there was no lock on it. A moonbeam lay across the hard-packed dirt floor, reaching almost to the bunk in which Merritt lay. He watched that beam of light. It was about two inches wide. Then he noticed that it was getting wider, very slowly, almost imperceptibly. It was three inches wide now, and growing.

Carefully, making no sound, Merritt reached for his gun belt, hanging from a hook on the bunk above him. The Colt gun slid out of the holster noiselessly.

Now the moonbeam was four inches wide, and it had stopped growing. He was up on one elbow, the gun in his hand, listening carefully, thinking perhaps the wind had blown the door open a little wider, knowing that it could not have been Tom Morse. Morse would have walked in immediately to awaken him.

He heard a horse stamp outside and he sat up a little straighter on the bunk, knowing now that it was not Tom Morse, because Morse would have come in, and it was not his own horse, because the gray would have been put in the lean-to. This was a horse, which meant that someone was prowling around the bunkhouse.

The moonbeam started to widen again, and then he saw the shadow come into it, a man's hat, flat-crowned with a wide rim, and then a gun. He saw this on the floor in the moonbeam as it stretched out to fall across the foot of his bunk, leaving the upper part of his body in darkness.

The door was half open now, and he saw the gun coming through, the moonlight glinting on the steel barrel. He could see the shape of the man behind the gun, his body silhouetted against the moonlight. The gun was pointing in the direction of the bunk, following the moonbeam as it widened and widened.

He had his own gun steady in his hand, lined on the target. Then another figure appeared behind the first and then the moonlight fell full across him on the bunk. He squeezed gently on the trigger, hearing the sharp exclamation of the man in the doorway. His Colt gun roared, a fraction of a second before the other man's. He heard the bullet strike the edge of the bunk above him, tearing splinters from the wood.

Then he was out of the bunk, firing at the second man, who had leaped to one side. He thought he saw a third figure back there in the shadows, too, but he was not sure of this. He fired twice at the doorsill, and then far in the distance he heard Tom Morse's whoop.

The first man coming through the doorway had pitched forward on the floor and was lying across the patch of moonlight. His hat had fallen from his head as he went down, and he was not moving. He lay on his face, his left arm doubled under him, his right arm outstretched, the gun still in his hand.

Merritt moved toward the doorway slowly. He

heard horses thrashing through the brush behind the bunkhouse, and then he ran outside in his socks.

He heard Tom Morse coming up from the direction of the herd, and Morse was yelling, "Merritt—you all right?"

"All right," Merritt said in a flat voice. He watched Morse ride up to the bunkhouse and throw himself out of the saddle.

"Who were they?" the tall man asked grimly.

"Reckon the same three that tried to work on me in the stable tonight," Merritt said slowly. "They came to finish the job."

"Damn 'em," Morse rasped. "All three of 'em?"

"Only two now," Merritt murmured. "One's inside."

Tom Morse looked at him. He said, "Maybe this one will talk, Merritt."

"I don't think so," Merritt said.

They went in, and Tom Morse lit the lamp again. The man Merritt had shot had not moved from his position. Morse rolled him over and stared at him curiously. He was dead, shot through the middle. There was a big, dark stain just above his belt.

Morse said curiously, "Know him?"

Merritt nodded. The man on the floor was the fellow with the black beard he'd seen at the surveyor's camp, one of the two men who'd fired the ranchhouse.

"This one ain't talkin'," Tom Morse observed.

"Not to me," Merritt Kane murmured. He was thinking that this was it now. Blood had been spilled a second time; this was war.

CHAPTER ELEVEN

IN THE MORNING Morse said, "Reckon we'll have to ride in an' tell Sheriff Tragan about this chap, Merritt."

Merritt looked at him across the fire they'd built outside the cabin, and over which they were boiling water for coffee. "We'll tell him," Merritt said, "if he needs to know."

"Reckon he's the law," Tom Morse said, and he looked at Merritt curiously.

"I'll ride in," Merritt said. "I'm expecting a wire, anyway."

Morse nodded. "Mightn't be too much trouble with this herd any more now, Merritt. Reckon they know we mean business."

"They weren't after the herd last night," Merritt said quietly. "They were after me."

"Why?" Morse asked bluntly.

"I might know," Merritt said, "when I receive that wire."

He rode in immediately after breakfast, and on the way he came up behind Sabine Bell, who was driving into town in the buckboard. She nodded to him as he came up, and then she stared at his face.

She said slowly, "What happened to you?"

"Had a little trouble in Broken Bow," Merritt

147

told her, "and then I shot a man last night who was sneaking into the bunkhouse with a gun in his hand."

Sabine slowed down the horses. "They were out to kill you?" she asked, her voice incredulous.

Merritt nodded. "He fired after my bullet struck him," he said briefly. "Came in at one o'clock in the morning without knocking."

"But why?" Sabine asked.

Merritt shrugged. "He didn't talk much after he was hit," he said. "One of the two chaps who burned me out the other morning. I tabbed them in the Wild West Saloon."

He told her of McGee's message, and the meeting with the two surveyor's men, and then the encounter in the stable.

Sabine said when he'd finished, "They wanted to kill you because you knew about them and they had to cover up."

"Why did they burn me out in the first place?" Merritt asked quietly.

Sabine looked at him, and shook her head slowly. "What are you going to do?" she asked.

"Figured I'd ride over to that surveyor's camp," Merritt told her, "and see if they're still around."

"They're not," Sabine told him. "One of my boys came in this morning with the news that they'd left last night. I guess the survey is through."

"They never reached Broken Bow," Merritt stated. "Why should it be through?"

"Mr. Dunstan of Great Kansas can tell you more about that than I can," Sabine said. "Ask him."

They rode on in silence for a few moments, and then Merritt said, "I understand Mr. West is selling property in town now, selling pretty fast."

Sabine glanced at him. "That's right," she said. "I suppose he feels this is the time to sell, when the prices are highest."

Merritt nodded. He rode along, rubbing his chin a little, and then Sabine said to him curiously, "Why did you bring that up, Mr. Kane?"

Merritt shrugged. "Ever stop to think what would happen in this town if the railroad didn't come through?"

"Didn't come through?" Sabine repeated. "But it's coming through. Mr. Dunstan is here. They've made the survey and marked out the route."

"What would happen, though," Merritt persisted, "if it didn't come? What about people like the Widow Buckley, who bought a lot at a very high price on Fremonte Street, and from Stephen West, thinking that the railroad was coming and there would be a business boom?"

Sabine was looking at him steadily. "Those people would lose a lot of money," she said quietly.

"And Stephen West would make a lot," Merritt observed. "Reckon he stands to make a lot whether the road comes through or not. Isn't that right?"

Sabine said a little testily, "You're putting Stephen in a very poor light, Mr. Kane."

"He's put himself there," Merritt observed.

They were coming up to the telegraph office, and he felt the excitement beginning to move him. In a very few moments he would know, and he wondered what he would do when he knew. He hadn't really thought of that yet.

Nodding to Sabine, he turned over toward the office. The operator was inside, fumbling through a batch of telegrams. He looked up when Merritt came in, recognizing him immediately.

Merritt said to him, "A reply come through to my message to Chicago?"

"Sorry," the operator told him. "Your message never went through, Mr. Kane. Had trouble on the line east of Ridge Center. Lines blew down in a storm. We couldn't get anything through to Chicago."

Merritt frowned. He said, "Send it off as soon as you can."

He went out into the street and saw Fay Dunstan coming toward him, some packages under her arm. She was dressed in white this morning, a dazzling white, with a large picture hat. There was a touch of blue in her costume, a light blue ribbon in the hat to match the color of her eyes.

Merritt stepped aside and touched his hat to her.

She looked at his face and she said, "You—you must have had a little trouble, Mr. Kane."

"Horse trouble," Merritt stated. "I was kicked."

"You seem to be such an excellent horseman," Fay smiled. "I'm surprised."

"Was a little surprised myself," Merritt murmured dryly. He'd noticed that she was coming toward the telegraph office, and that was the last building on the street. He said, "If you're figuring on sending a message, Miss Dunstan, the lines are down. Wires can't get through."

The blue eyes clouded. She said thoughtfully, "I wanted to wire Mother that Peter and I wouldn't be going home as soon as we thought. Peter received a message from the company last night that he would be stationed here indefinitely. We—we hadn't expected that."

"I see," Merritt said. "If you leave your message, the operator will get it out as soon as the wires are cleared." He went on then, walking slowly up the street, his brow knit in thought.

Outside the Wild West, Jonathan West was chatting with Big Sam McGee. They saw him coming, and McGee waved a hand.

Young Jonathan was smiling when Merritt came up. He said, "Very sorry to hear of your trouble last night, Mr. Kane. Feeling all right now?"

"I'll have a headache for a year," Merritt said ruefully. To McGee he said, "What's new, Sam?"

"Finn Tragan's got himself a little help," McGee stated. "Came in on the mornin' stage."

"Help?" Merritt repeated.

"Swore in a deputy," McGee explained. "I guess Tragan figures things might be gettin' a little rough in this town when the road comes through. He's gettin' ready for it."

Merritt digested this fact. He said then, "Who is he?"

"Comin' up now," McGee said softly, and Merritt turned around.

Two men had just come out of the Comanche Saloon, and were moving up the street, walking without haste. The man on the inside was Finn Tragan, small, thin, his tiny hands hooked in his vest pockets.

The man with him, walking on the outside of the walk, was tall and golden-haired, with a mustache of the same golden color. His tall, well-built figure was dressed meticulously in fawn-colored pants and a black frock coat, which bulged on the right side where his gun was strapped. He wore a spotless gray vest with a heavy gold chain draped across it. His cravat was maroon and cream, and his shirt was of the finest broadcloth, spotless white.

Sam McGee said softly, "A dude if I ever see one."

Merritt was staring at this tall man in the immaculate dress, recognizing him immediately, and as he recognized Tragan's new deputy he also remembered Tragan, because these two had once gone together.

The deputy was smiling affably as he walked. His new boots were highly polished, as if they'd just come out of the box. He wore a pearl-gray hat with a broad rim and a tiny red feather stuck in the band.

Two young girls came out of a store nearby, and they stared at the new deputy as he went by. One of them laughed, but they were both impressed, and Merritt Kane was thinking that they should be, because the man with the golden mustache was Handsome Billy Deal, professional gambler, professional lady's man, and professional killer from El Paso, Texas.

The man with him, who posed as Finn Tragan, sheriff of Broken Bow, was the El Paso Kid, as murderous a killer as ever walked the streets of a southwestern town. Years before, Merritt had passed through El Paso, and he'd had these two men pointed out to him. He hadn't stayed in El Paso very long, and he was not there on business, but he'd seen the El Paso Kid in action during that very brief stay. He'd seen the Kid shoot down a man in one of the El Paso saloons, and he remembered what the Kid could do with a six-gun.

They were coming straight toward the three on the porch, and then the El Paso Kid saw Merritt. He slowed down almost imperceptibly, and he said something to Billy Deal. Deal glanced at Merritt curiously, and Merritt noticed the color of his eyes, a flinty gray color, dead eyes, merciless eyes that spoiled his handsome face.

The Kid said, "Gentlemen, meet William Deal, our new deputy." He introduced the three men on the porch.

Deal stood back, nodding pleasantly. He shook hands with no one, but he watched Merritt carefully, studying him as he stood on the porch with Sam McGee and young West. His gray eyes were veiled, revealing nothing.

His voice when he spoke was soft, almost refined. He said, "Glad to know you, gentlemen. Trust we'll get along."

"Shouldn't have any trouble," Sam McGee murmured.

"Anything you have to tell me," the El Paso Kid purred, "you can tell Billy Deal."

Merritt said quietly, "I'll tell both of you. I shot a man out at my place last night when he tried to sneak into my house with a gun in his hand."

He heard Jonathan West's gasp of surprise, and then the sheriff of Broken Bow said, "Who was it, Kane?"

"Saw him with that survey crew in the valley," Merritt said. "He worked with them."

The Kid looked at Billy Deal, and there was the suggestion of a grin on his face. He said blandly, "Maybe stealin', Billy. He went in there to rob."

"Rob what?" Merritt asked tersely.

The Kid shrugged, but said nothing.

Billy Deal murmured, "Would you call it self-defense, Mr. Kane?"

Merritt looked at him. "He came into my place," he said. "I didn't go into his."

"Who fired the first shot?" Deal persisted.

Merritt's eyes hardened. He had the feeling that these two men were mocking him, playing with him. He said quietly, "If I hadn't fired the first shot I wouldn't be talking to you now."

"Always shoot first," Handsome Billy Deal murmured. "It's safer."

Merritt had started to take a cigar from his vest pocket. He put it back now, and his voice was brittle when he spoke. He said softly, "Deal, this town pay you to make remarks like that?"

Billy Deal shrugged. "Reckon that was just a little personal observation, Mr. Kane," he purred.

"Keep it to yourself," Merritt snapped. He saw Sam McGee flash him a warning look, but he ignored it. He was beginning to boil inside now. That shot from the dark alley, the attack in the stable, the attempted murder as he lay in his bunk, the burning of his ranchhouse; these things had been working on him for days, and he was ready to blow. This tall, golden-haired man with the sneer in his voice was goading him.

He wondered for a moment how far Handsome Billy Deal would go in this matter. There was the possibility that Deal was only testing him, seeing what he was made of, and filing this knowledge away for future reference. On the other hand, Deal might have been ordered to work on him immediately.

Deal said, "You're a little testy this morning, my friend."

"I asked you to keep your remarks to yourself," Merritt said ominously.

Billy Deal looked at him, that thin smile glued to his face. He said softly, "Always safer to shoot first, Mr. Kane."

Merritt went off the porch in one long bound, swinging his fist at Deal's face. He hit hard and savagely, and he heard the short cry escape from Deal's mouth as the tall man staggered backward, his hat falling from his head.

He stumbled back against the Kid, and he was reaching for his gun inside his coat when Merritt caught up with him again. As Merritt had anticipated, Deal did not like to work with his fists. A man who dressed like that did not like to grovel in the dirt.

Deal's gun was half out of the holster when Merritt hit him again and again, sending him spinning out into the dust of the road. The gun slipped from his hands as he bounced against one of the posts of the hitching rail, caromed off it, and fell down in the dust.

Merritt heard Sam McGee say behind him,

"One fight, Mr. Tragan. Just one fight, an' two men in it."

As Deal got up out of the dust, blood trickling from his cut mouth, his eyes murderous, the crowd started to gather. Deal did not like to fight with his fists, but he was not a coward, and he was a big man.

Merritt kicked his gun away and unbuckled his own gun belt, draping it across the hitching rail. He saw Sabine Bell come out of a store across the road, and then Fay Dunstan came up from the telegraph office. He wished Fay would not see this, because it was not going to be pleasant.

Billy Deal took off his black coat, dusted it automatically, and draped it across the hitching rail. He said slowly, "You wanted a fight, Mr. Kane. Come and get it."

Merritt walked toward him, and Deal knocked him down with a vicious punch to the side of the neck. Merritt fell on hands and knees, shook his head once, and got up to meet Deal's second charge. He saw the punches coming, and he lowered his head, ducked in under them, and started to hammer at Deal's stomach, digging his boots into the soft dust of the road and driving forward. He hit hard, savagely, and he heard Deal gasp from the impact of the blows.

Deal went down in the center of the road and Merritt stumbled over him, falling also. Both men got up slowly, without haste, knowing that this would be a long fight, not decided by one punch.

The crowd gathered quickly, but they made little noise as crowds usually did at a fight. Circling his man, Merritt saw Sam McGee and Jonathan West still on the porch. The Kid was standing on the step below them, watching passively.

Stephen West was there, too, having crossed over from his office. He was wearing his vest but no coat, and his sleeves were rolled up. He came up and stood beside Sabine Bell on the walk. Fay Dunstan had stopped a dozen feet from the two, and she was looking across at the fighters.

Billy Deal came in swinging big fists, a slightly taller man than Merritt, but not as heavy in the shoulders. Merritt met him with a swinging punch to the mouth, and the blood started to gush from between Deal's loosened teeth. He shook his head and tore in again, hitting hard for Merritt's face. One punch got through to the right cheek, and Merritt felt the slash of it. The punch had not been particularly hard, but Deal was wearing a large gold ring on that hand, and the ring slashed the cheek open.

Merritt felt the blood dripping from his chin, and he saw Fay Dunstan turn her head away. Sabine Bell was watching almost calmly, but her hands were tight at her sides.

They stood toe to toe for a few moments, hitting

at each other, and then Deal closed in, grappled Merritt around the waist, and tried to throw him to the ground. At the same time he brought his left knee up into Merritt's groin, staggering him so that he went down on hands and knees.

He was aiming a kick at Merritt's face with his boot when Big Sam McGee, who'd pushed his way up to the inner circle now, stuck out his own hard shoe, blocking the kick. McGee said, "Not in this fight, Deal."

Merritt got up, feeling the effects of that vicious kick, feeling the pain in his head from the gash he'd got the night before. He wondered how long he could keep up a fight like this, and then he looked into Billy Deal's face, seeing the exhaustion there, too.

Deal stood about three feet away from him, panting, his face battered, bruised, bleeding from the nose and mouth. His beautiful gray vest was a mess. His fawn-colored pants were torn at the knees. Seeing him in this battered condition gave Merritt heart.

He moved in, smiling a little, and that smile seemed to take the fight out of Handsome Billy Deal. For the first time Deal backed away a little without being hit. Merritt followed him, but not for long. Deal suddenly lunged in again, smashing his right fist at Merritt's face.

Merritt ducked a little, dug his left into Deal's stomach, and then hit him again in the same place with the right hand. He felt the fist go deep into the soft flesh of Deal's stomach, and he knew that the fight was over.

Deal bent over, gasping for breath. He'd been backed up against the hitching rail, and he stood there now, grasping the rail with his left hand, clutching his stomach with his right, his face green. He was an open target, and everyone in the crowd could see it.

Merritt looked at him for a moment, rubbed his hands on his trouser legs, and then turned and pushed back through the crowd. He heard a faint cheer go up from the crowd as he pushed into the Wild West Saloon, Sam McGee at his heels. There had been no cheering all the way. Men did not cheer at a fight like that.

McGee led him to a back room in the saloon, sat him down on a chair, and then went out. He came back with a basin of water and a towel, and he said regretfully, "Again, Merritt."

"I'll hire you," Merritt murmured, "as my personal physician."

"That's a nasty gash on the cheek," McGee muttered as he went to work on Merritt's battered face.

Jonathan West came in, stood inside the entrance-way, and said, "Anything I can do, Mr. Kane?"

"Where's Deal?" Merritt asked him.

"They took him into the Comanche," young West said. "He's pretty well done in."

"Some of them punches," Sam McGee said, "would have done in anybody, my friend." He said to Merritt, "One more fight like this, Kane, and they'll bury you."

"Reckon I'll try to get a rest in between," Merritt told him.

He wondered now what he'd accomplished by the fight. Some of the tension had gone out of him, and that was good. He'd blown off steam, but he'd made a bad enemy in Handsome Billy Deal. Deal was a man with pride, a vain man, and a man like that never in this world forgot an affront. He'd been humbled before a big crowd in this town, and he would not rest until he'd paid off the debt.

A man came into the room, smoking a cigar. He said, "Deal's in the Comanche, Kane."

"That right?" Merritt murmured.

"He says the next time don't try to use your fists on him," the man stated. "He says come shootin', mister."

Merritt nodded. "I'll remember it," he said.

Jonathan West, standing in the room, looked a little pale. He said slowly, when the messenger had gone out, "We're going to have trouble in this town, Mr. Kane."

"Reckon I've known that," Merritt said grimly, "for a long time, Jonathan."

CHAPTER TWELVE

AFTER SAM MCGEE patched him up as best he could, reducing the swellings on his face with cold-water applications, Merritt lay on the cot in the rear room for another hour or so, recovering his strength. He'd used up more energy than he'd thought in that encounter with Deal, and the affair the previous evening hadn't helped.

McGee said, "Take a little sleep. Nobody's comin' in here. That Deal chap won't be in condition to walk for another couple of hours if he did want to come an' look you up."

"I don't like to leave Morse out at my place alone," Merritt said. "Not for too long a time, anyway."

"Nobody will run off stock in the daytime," McGee said. "You can spot 'em too easily."

Merritt had his rest, and he stayed in town for his dinner, eating in the hotel restaurant, as usual. He felt much better after the meal, but his face and body were still terribly sore. He didn't feel quite up to riding out to the ranch immediately, and he sat on the porch for a spell, just letting his long frame relax in the chair. He lit a cigar and smoked it, listening to the sounds of the quiet afternoon.

A dog loped by, tongue lolling, glancing up at

him as it went by. Two men came out of the hotel, discussing a deal they'd just made with Stephen West for the purchase of a lot on Main Street. Merritt heard the words "Thousand dollars a foot."

Sam McGee had been right about the price of real estate in Broken Bow. Merritt looked at his cigar. He watched the two men walk down the street, and then he heard a door slam diagonally across the road.

Sabine Bell, face pale and tight, had slammed the door of Stephen West's office and was coming across the road, walking stiffly, shoulders erect. West had come to the door and was watching her through the glass partition, a cigar in his mouth, and then he went away.

Sabine was on the walk in front of the hotel, moving past the porch in the direction of her buckboard, which was tied a few doors down. Seeing Merritt in the chair, she came over and stood below him, knowing that he'd seen her come out of the office.

Merritt moistened his lips. He said, "Slamming doors won't help any, ma'am."

Sabine's eyes were still blazing. "We had an argument," she admitted. "I asked him about the railroad. I—I've been thinking a lot since I left you."

Merritt nodded. "What did he have to say?" he asked curiously.

"Said it wasn't any of his business if the road

came through or not," Sabine scowled. "He was in the real-estate business. He was selling land. He told me to see Dunstan if I had any questions."

Merritt smiled a little. "Have any questions?"

Sabine looked at him grimly. "Some," she said. "I asked him what would happen to all the people who are buying property in this town if the railroad didn't come through. I asked him about Jim Holbrook, the dry goods man. He just bought a lot from Paramount Realty, and he intends to put up a two-story building with a warehouse in the rear. Holbrook is investing every penny he has, and he's borrowing from the bank in order to go through with the deal."

Merritt puffed on the cigar, watching the girl's face, letting her go on because he knew that it was good for her to get it off her chest.

"We had words," Sabine finished. "Stephen said these are business deals, and a man knows he's taking a risk in any business deal."

"Those chaps have been told the road is coming through," Merritt observed. "They've seen the surveyors and they've seen and heard Dunstan. Great Kansas has an office in this town. They don't figure it's a risk at all."

Sabine didn't say anything. She stood there, staring down the street for a few moments, watching a rider come on, move past, leaving a little cloud of yellow dust hanging in the air, the sun glinting on the particles.

"You buy cattle," Merritt said, "and you know what you have. You can tell a good head from a bad one. Land is different. It's land, and it's worth a dollar a foot or a thousand a foot, depending upon where it is and what can be done with it. West is right that you have to be careful buying land."

"There's the matter of personal honesty involved, too," Sabine said slowly. "A man expects his neighbor to be honest with him."

Merritt didn't say anything to that. He permitted the thought to hang there in the air. Then Sabine nodded to him and walked on to the buckboard, but she walked more slowly now, as if in deep thought. Merritt watched her ride out of town.

It was nearly three o'clock in the afternoon when he felt rested enough to start back to the ranch. He still ached all over, though, when he stepped into the saddle and turned the gray south out of town.

On the other side of the draw, moving parallel with the Double Bell range, he saw a rider angling toward him out of the hills. He slowed down, noticing that the rider was coming directly toward him, intercepting him. Then his eyes widened a little as he recognized Fay Dunstan.

She was riding a chestnut mare she'd probably hired from the stable. She had on an eastern riding costume and her boots were new and shiny. She was a good horsewoman.

Merritt watched her as she topped a small rise and came down into the road beside him. She was smiling pleasantly, but he had the vague feeling that he should be careful with this girl. She was Dunstan's sister, and Dunstan and Stephen West were very close. West had brought in the El Paso Kid.

These things, added up, might mean nothing as far as Fay was concerned. Very possibly she had no inkling of the business going on in Broken Bow. She was Dunstan's sister, and she'd come out here for a vacation. She had been very pleasant right from the beginning.

"I'm surprised," Fay smiled, "that you're able to ride after that affair in town this morning."

"A man gets over that," Merritt told her. He felt of his bruised face tenderly.

"What was it about?" Fay asked him curiously. "It seemed strange to see two grown men fighting like small boys."

Merritt shrugged. "We had words," he said. "In this country men fight over words."

Fay Dunstan shook her head, perplexed. "It's a strange country," she admitted, "but I love it." She looked at him rather archly. "I've been itching to see a little of it since coming out here, but Peter is always so very busy, and Mr. West is—is engaged, I understand. I came out alone this afternoon. You don't mind if I ride along with you?"

Merritt shrugged. "Just heading out to the ranch," he told her. He added thoughtfully, "Seems like a damn-fool business having a woman take me home, though."

Fay laughed gaily. "If you're not too worn out," she said, "we could make a little diversion." She pointed toward two pink buttes rising up above the encircling hills, and she said, "I'd started to ride in that direction when I saw you coming. They—they're quite beautiful. I'd like to get a closer look at them."

Merritt stared at the distant buttes. They were about a half-dozen miles to the east, away from the Double Bell range. He'd noticed them on his way to and from Broken Bow.

"Of course if you're too tired," Fay said a little reluctantly, "after that affair with that dreadful man—"

Merritt stared at the buttes. "Reckon we can get a little closer," he stated, and the smile came again to her face. He was glad that he had said it. He fancied that she might have been quite lonely in this strange town with not too many eligible men around. The fact that she'd gone out riding alone was proof of this.

They left the stage road, moving up into the hills, Fay leading the way, and Merritt noticing that she rode very well indeed.

He said, "They have good riding academies in the East, Miss Dunstan."

"I've been riding for a number of years," Fay said, "and this chestnut is perfect."

They dipped down below the hills, their horses splashing through a tiny, pebbly stream, and then they climbed another grade, dipping down into a valley where the heat lay heavy and still, the heat devils dancing in the distance.

Overhead an eagle circled endlessly in the blue vault of the sky. Merritt's jaw was aching, and his ribs still hurt from the fight. He almost wished now that he'd accepted the excuse of the fight and gone on out to the ranch. He'd left Tom Morse back there alone, and he did not like that too much, even though it did not seem possible that anyone would molest them in the daytime.

This was a land of huge rocks and boulders, of rocks standing black and ominous against the sky on the ridges of the hills, balanced there precariously.

A lizard scurried around the base of a rock, and Fay, riding a few feet ahead of Merritt, moving between the scattered rocks on the valley floor, let out a short cry of alarm. She glanced back at him as if a little ashamed, and then she rode on.

They paused for a drink when the little stream turned their way again, and then they rode to the top of the next ridge, pausing here because they could see the buttes again.

Ahead of them was another long, narrow valley, strewn with big boulders, extending directly toward the buttes. Merritt assumed they had gone far enough, and he was ready and willing to turn back, but Fay with a light laugh let the chestnut move down the slope.

Merritt frowned and went after her. Between the boulders for a distance of about a half mile was a patch of hard, firm soil, almost like a race track set out before them.

Fay Dunstan glanced back at Merritt, waved a hand, and then let the chestnut break out into a sharp trot, riding away from him like a schoolgirl, her hair flying behind her.

Merritt followed more slowly, and he was thinking of Sabine Bell, comparing her to Fay Dunstan. Sabine he understood; this girl ahead of him, he was not sure. Off to his right he heard the warning buzz of a rattlesnake. The gray leaped forward a little, and as it did so a rifle cracked from the slope to Merritt's right. Then another banged from the opposite slope, the bullet striking the saddle horn, glancing off.

Face taut, Merritt whipped out his Colt gun, whirled the gray, and sprinted for the protection of a clump of boulders twenty-five yards to his rear and slightly up the slope on the right side.

The two rifles followed him, and each marksman got off two shots before he made the boulders. He'd been caught between the dreaded cross fire. Sliding off the gray, he plunged in among the boulders and started to work his way up toward the man on the slope. He had to work fast and keep behind protecting boulders all the time because the man on the slope was trying to catch him in the open.

Halfway up the slope he caught a glimpse of a man among the rocks. The rifleman was peering forward, trying to see him. Merritt raced across an open space, diving behind another high boulder just as the rifle cracked from across the little valley, and the slug gouged a hole in the dirt behind him.

He hadn't fired a single shot yet, but he was within thirty or forty yards of the man on this side of the valley, and that was close enough. He started to wriggle forward on his stomach, moving in and out among the rocks, knowing that he had some small advantage now. The man above him did not quite know where he was or in what direction he was coming up the slope. The whole side of the valley here was strewn with huge rocks and boulders, giving him plenty of protection as he went up.

He bore toward the right, making a wide circuit that eventually brought him to the summit of the valley wall. Neither rifle had spoken for some time now, indicating that they'd lost track of him. He crawled forward, inching closer and closer to his prey all the time.

Then he stopped and listened carefully. He hadn't heard anything from Fay Dunstan. She'd been quite a distance ahead when the shots had been fired, and he hadn't particularly worried about her because the men on the slopes were after him.

Then he thought about Fay Dunstan again as he lay on his stomach among the rocks here, the hot sun beating down on his back, and the thoughts were not pleasant. He told himself that it could not be, and yet there was the possibility. He remembered now that she'd done most of the leading on this little ride. She'd suggested the direction, and she'd kept riding off ahead of him, displaying a knowledge of this country that she could not possibly possess unless she'd been out here before, but she claimed that she had not been outside of Broken Bow since arriving.

When those shots had been fired from the slopes she'd been a safe distance ahead, and she'd turned to wave to him. Could that wave of the hand have been a signal for someone else— for men concealed up on the slopes with deadly rifles?

Merritt started to move forward again, and then he caught a glimpse of the marksman on this side, and recognized him. The man was the pock-marked fellow he'd pushed into the livery stable behind the Wild West Saloon, the same man who'd fired his ranch for reasons known only to himself.

The rifleman was about twenty-five yards ahead

of him, crouched behind a rock, still peering down the slope, his rifle in readiness. Even from that distance Merritt could see that the man was terribly nervous. He was licking his lips, rubbing the barrel of the rifle, and then glancing across at the opposite slope.

Flat on his stomach, Merritt picked up a small rock on the ground in front of him. Raising himself slightly, he tossed the rock at the pock-marked man. It struck the boulder against which he was leaning, and he spun around, the fear of death in his eyes.

Merritt was up on his feet now, standing behind a huge boulder that protected him from the other rifleman. He had his gun in his hand, and the gun was steady on the target.

The pock-marked man yelled, almost screamed. He swung his rifle around, fumbled with it, and then took Merritt's first shot in the chest. He staggered back to a sitting position, his hat falling from his head, and he sat there, trying to maneuver the rifle, doing it the way a small child would twist a toy gun around in its hands, not certain just what to do with it. Then he fell over backward.

Merritt clicked the empty shell out of the cylinder, put in a fresh one, and peered out around the edge of the boulder. He could hear a horse moving away from the other slope, running hard, and he caught a glimpse of the rifleman who'd been there, riding away, moving east in the direction of Broken Bow. At the distance he could not identify the man.

He walked up to the pock-marked man, looked down at him for a moment, and then turned and strode down the slope. He saw Fay Dunstan riding toward him when he reached the boulders where he'd left the horse. She was calling, "Mr. Kane—Mr. Kane!"

Merritt mounted and rode over to her. He noticed that she was pale and agitated.

She gasped, "What—what happened, Mr. Kane? I heard the shooting."

"Ambush," Merritt said briefly. "Somebody was waiting for me, Miss Dunstan. Reckon we'd better head back to town now. I'll go in with you."

"But who were they?" she persisted.

"People who didn't like me," Merritt murmured, "and figured I'd be better off dead than alive." He didn't say any more on the subject. They rode back to Broken Bow, stopping in front of the livery stable alley where Fay had hired her horse.

Fay said, "You'll notify Sheriff Tragan about this, won't you, Mr. Kane?"

"I'll think about it," Merritt told her dryly. "We had a nice ride, Miss Dunstan."

She looked at him carefully, but his face revealed nothing. Then she rode into the alley with the horse, and Merritt headed the gray out of town. He passed the telegraph office, and he saw the operator standing in the doorway. To his questioning look the man shook his head, indicating that messages weren't going through yet.

It was late afternoon when Merritt pushed the gray up the slope and out of the draw. He was anxious to get back now, regretting the fact that he'd left Tom Morse alone so long.

He was moving up into the timber beyond Double Bell when he heard the rider hammering toward him, coming down through the break in the woods. The man was a Double Bell rider whom he'd seen in town before.

Seeing Merritt coming up, he drew rein quickly, his face hard. He said, "Just ridin' in for you, Kane. Miss Bell sent me. Your man Morse was shot this afternoon—shot dead."

CHAPTER THIRTEEN

MERRITT FOUND THEM up on the slope about a quarter of a mile from the bunkhouse. He'd learned on the way that his stock had been run off, and Morse had been shot as he tried to hold them back.

Sabine Bell was there, and about a half-dozen Double Bell riders. Tom Morse lay where he'd fallen, but they'd put a tarpaulin over his body. Merritt could see his boots sticking out from beneath the tarpaulin. He dismounted and walked over to look down at the body for a moment. Then he went over to Sabine.

She said briefly, "One of our boys is part Indian and the best tracker in these parts. He told us what happened."

"What happened?" Merritt asked quietly.

"There were four of them," Sabine said, "according to the sign. Two of them jumped your herd and started toward the south with it. Tom must have been at the bunkhouse. He went after them, riding into a trap set by two others who were lying hidden in the brush on either side of this spot. They caught Tom in a cross fire as he came through."

"Cross fire," Merritt repeated slowly. He'd

been lucky because a rattler had sounded at him. Tom Morse's luck had run out.

"He was hit twice," Sabine said. "That was enough. Either bullet would have done it."

"What about the stock?" Merritt asked.

"Two of our boys trailed the herd," Sabine murmured. "They just came in with a report. Your stock was driven over a precipice three miles from here. Your hundred and fifty head are lying at the base of a hundred-foot cliff. I suppose they've stopped moaning now."

"So we'll never know who did it," Merritt said slowly. "They'll ride in to Broken Bow the way the others did who burned my place."

Sabine Bell looked at him, a peculiar look in her eyes. She said, "We know who did it, Merritt. Morse didn't die right away."

"You talked to him?" Merritt asked quickly.

Sabine shook her head. "He was dead when we got here. We'd heard the shots in the distance and we came to look. He was dead, but he'd left a message on the ground." She stopped.

Merritt looked at her and then went back to the dead form sprawled under the tarpaulin. He lifted it slightly up where the head was. Morse had fallen in soft dirt here. With a piece of twig he'd scrawled something in the dirt.

Turning his head slightly, Merritt read it. It was a scrawl, the writing of a man who was dying, but it was legible. It was one word; it said, "Tragan."

Replacing the tarpaulin, Merritt came back to the group. There was no emotion in his voice when he spoke. He said, "Tragan was behind the burning of my place, and he's been with the bunch trying to shoot me down."

"Why?" Sabine asked.

"I have an idea," Merritt told her. "I might know in a matter of hours."

Sabine Bell watched his face closely. She said, "I sent one of our boys in for Joe Brockton, the undertaker. He'll come out for Tom. You'd better come with us. Tragan won't run away."

"No," Merritt smiled thinly. "He won't run away."

"You're going after him," Sabine said.

Merritt nodded, and Sabine said, "Now he has a deputy with him—another gun."

"That's all right," Merritt said.

Sabine didn't say any more on the subject. They rode off, heading in the direction of Double Bell, and when they reached there it was almost dusk.

"I'll make coffee," Sabine said. "Sit down."

It was the first time Merritt had been inside the house. It was very comfortable, nicely furnished, with a woman's taste. There were curtains across the windows and Indian rugs on the floor, and it was spotlessly clean.

He went out in the kitchen and he sat down at the table there, feeling more at home in that room. He watched Sabine bustling around the room, and he sat there, twisting his hat around and around in his hands, thinking of the cross fire into which Tom Morse had ridden, and the ambush they'd laid for him in the Yellow Hills.

Sabine said to him, "Are you cleaned out?"

Merritt looked at the floor. "I have a little cash left," he said. "Not too much. I might be able to borrow money and stock up again." He wasn't thinking of those things now. He had other business to attend to first—the business of Finn Tragan, the El Paso Kid, other business.

He drank the coffee Sabine set down before him, and he watched her take a seat on the opposite side of the table. He wondered how many times Stephen West had sat in this chair in the kitchen, and the thought disturbed him.

Sabine said, "Enjoy your ride this afternoon, Merritt?"

Merritt smiled mirthlessly. "I was set up," he said. "Ran into the same kind of cross fire Tom Morse hit."

Sabine leaned forward, staring at him. Merritt said, "I got one of them. Other chap got away."

"Miss Dunstan there?" Sabine asked.

Merritt looked at her. "She was there," he stated, "up ahead of me when they opened fire."

Sabine shook her head, puzzled. She watched Merritt drink his coffee, and when he finished he got up.

He said, "Reckon I'll ride in."

"They'll set you up again," Sabine told him. "You'll ride right into it. They know you're coming now."

"That's all right," Merritt said.

"I'm bringing Double Bell in," Sabine said quietly. "I can do that much to see that you get a fair deal."

"You're asking for trouble," Merritt said. "Why?"

Sabine shrugged. "You rode in here looking for peace," she said. "You've run into a lot of trouble not of your asking. I've seen that much. Now you're a neighbor."

Merritt nodded. "I don't want to get your boys in trouble," he said. "I'd like it better if they weren't in town."

"They'll be in town," Sabine said flatly, and there was no arguing with her.

Merritt got up, murmured his thanks for the coffee, and headed for the door.

Sabine followed him out on the porch and watched him get into the saddle. She called after him, "Be careful."

He couldn't see her face in the shadows there, but he thought he detected a note of concern in her voice. He rode slowly, deep in thought.

On the main stage road he passed Joe Brockton's undertaker's wagon taking in the body of Tom Morse, and as he went past the wagon he was thinking raggedly that if he'd been present Morse might not have died.

The stars were shining overhead as he approached Broken Bow. He slowed down at the top of the draw, looking down at the town, the yellow lights forming that ragged line which was Main Street. It was cool now on top of the draw. He listened, but it was very quiet in Broken Bow. A child cried from one of the nearer houses. Over on the slope the schoolhouse was a dark square against the night sky.

Merritt moved down the grade and into town. He stopped by the telegraph office, dismounted, and went inside.

The operator nodded to him pleasantly, but there was a strange expression on his face. He said before Merritt could speak, "Your message went through, Mr. Kane, and the reply came in fifteen minutes ago."

Merritt hunched over the counter, saying nothing, as the operator went through a batch of papers, picked out the wire he'd just received, and placed it on the wood in front of Merritt. He also placed beside this sheet a copy of the message Merritt had sent.

"I—I couldn't help knowing what's in the message," the operator muttered. "It came through on the wire, Mr. Kane."

"I know," Merritt said. He studied the short message carefully, and then he folded both of them together and placed them in his shirt pocket. Rolling a cigarette, he eyed the man thoughtfully, and he said, "Anybody see this message? You tell anybody about it yet?"

"Nobody's been here," the operator said.

"All right. Keep it to yourself till tomorrow morning," Merritt told him.

"Anything you say, Mr. Kane," the young man murmured, but he was still a little worried. He scratched his chin, and then he said, "I—I suppose you know Mr. West saw that message you sent out, Mr. Kane."

Merritt had turned and was starting for the door. He stopped slowly and swung around. He said, "West?"

The operator was ill at ease. "Mr. West told me you'd asked him to check over the message before I sent it out," he muttered. "You did, didn't you?"

"No," Merritt said. He was smiling grimly now, seeing the parts beginning to fit together at long last. He said, "So West saw it?"

"I showed it to him," the operator nodded. "He just said that it was all right the way it was."

"Did he see the reply to my wire?" Merritt wanted to know.

"He never came back," the operator said. "That was about three o'clock this afternoon. I got the wire through a few minutes later."

Merritt went out and stepped into the saddle.

Only one person knew he'd sent off a wire, and that person was Fay Dunstan. She'd seen him coming out of the telegraph office, and she'd relayed the message on to Stephen West. West had been so curious about that message that he'd lied to the operator about it in order to read its contents. Now West knew, and Merritt wondered what he would do.

He watched the road on both sides as he walked the gray down the street. He went past Finn Tragan's office, noting that the light was out and the padlock on the door. He looked over the batwing doors of several saloons as he passed them, searching for Tragan and Deal, but he saw neither of them.

The northbound stage hammered down out of the draw at about the time Joe Brockton's wagon came in. Dismounting in front of the Wild West, Merritt watched it whirl by and pull up in front of the stage office up the street.

He went into the Wild West, and it was early evening, only a few customers in the house. Big Sam McGee was having his supper at a table in the corner, a boy having brought a tray from the restaurant. He waved to Merritt with a fork, and Merritt went over that way.

"Heard about Tom Morse," McGee scowled. "Tough, Merritt."

"It was tough," Merritt said.

"Know who did it?" McGee asked him, and

Merritt realized then that Sabine Bell had given orders to her riders not to tell of the message the dying Tom Morse had left in the dirt where he'd fallen.

"I know who did it," Merritt said evenly.

Sam McGee looked at him. He continued to eat, but he didn't say any more.

Merritt said, "Tragan or Deal been around, Sam?"

"Ain't seen 'em," McGee stated, and his eyes widened a little. "Tragan?" he repeated.

"Tragan," Merritt nodded. He leaned against the wall, facing the door, watching that door all the time.

Sam McGee ate thoughtfully, slowly. Then he said, "Saw Tragan about an hour ago down near the hotel, Merritt. He ain't been up this way, though."

Merritt nodded. He thought bitterly, Tragan and West and Dunstan, and maybe Asa Creel, too, but he wasn't sure about Asa Creel, the banker. There was a good chance that they were all at the hotel, up in Dunstan's room, talking this thing over, making their plans. He had another quick thought, and he was surprised that he hadn't thought of that before. They would be waiting for that return wire to come in, knowing that when he had that he'd know everything. Now they thought he was only guessing. They'd want to see that wire when it came in.

Possibly they'd try to get it before he could get it.

Pushing away from the wall, Merritt said, "That side door lead into the alley, Sam?" He nodded toward a door to the right of the bar.

McGee nodded. He looked at Merritt closely. Merritt said, "You don't know where I went, Sam. That right?"

"I don't know nothin'," McGee nodded. "Go ahead."

Merritt crossed the room, pushed open the door, and stepped into the alley there. He didn't go out to Main Street, but headed the other way, toward the rear of the building and the vacant lots back there.

Behind the livery stable in which he'd had the fight, he got his bearings and walked due north behind the row of buildings along Main Street. When he came to the last house, he made a wide circuit, climbed a low fence there, and then trotted across the road to the side on which the telegraph office was located.

The lights were on in the little one-story structure, and he could hear the instrument clacking away. He came up behind the house instead of going toward the front door. There was a shed behind the building, and a rear door leading to the shed.

Merritt came up behind the rear door, pushed gently, and opened it. He saw the operator sitting with his back to him, the phones over his ears, receiving messages.

Closing the door behind him, Merritt waited until the man had taken the phones off, and then he said, "I came back. Mind if I wait here?"

The operator stared at him in bewilderment, and Merritt said, "I had to come in the back door. There's a chance that someone is watching this place now. I don't know."

"Who are you waiting for?" the clerk asked.

"First man who asks to see a copy of the message I received tonight," Merritt told him calmly. He was thinking, They'll send Tragan down. He wears the star, and he can bluff his way through.

The operator licked his lips and shook his head. "Hard to believe yet," he said. "I don't understand it, Mr. Kane."

"Reckon you'd understand it," Merritt said tersely, "if you knew how much West and Dunstan and others were making on this deal."

The operator nodded. "I see the light," he said.

"Anybody come in here this afternoon, looking for the wire I expected?" Merritt wanted to know.

"Message only came through about a half hour ago," the operator said. "You expecting someone now?"

"It's a hunch," Merritt told him. He took the folded wire out of his shirt pocket, handed it to the operator, and said, "If they ask for it, give it to them, and then get out that back door."

The young man gulped a little. He nodded weakly as he accepted the yellow paper.

Merritt stepped away from the rear door, taking a seat in the corner where he could not be seen from the counter. He took off his hat and placed it on top of a cabinet. Then he slipped the Colt gun out of the holster, spun the cylinder, and slid it back again.

He was whistling tunelessly as the instrument began to clack again, and the operator sat down and put on the phones. Outside, he heard a group of riders swing by, entering town, and he wondered if they were Double Bell men.

After the operator had taken the message it became silent in the room again. Merritt leaned back in the chair, completely relaxed as if deep in thought. Not a muscle in his face moved. He took out a cigar, chewed off the tip, and lighted it.

The operator said, "Damn it, but you're cool, Mr. Kane. Who do you expect in here tonight?"

"Sheriff Tragan," Merritt told him calmly.

"Tragan?" the operator repeated. "He—he in on this?"

"Who got him in office?" Merritt countered.

The operator nodded. "It makes sense," he admitted.

The silence descended on the room again, and then they heard a step on the walk outside. The operator jumped, his face losing some color. He was standing at the counter, both hands flat on the wood as if steadying himself, when a man whom Merritt recognized as Holbrook, the storekeeper, came in.

Holbrook wrote out a message, handed it to the operator, and said, "Get this off quick, Ed. Order for lumber for my new building. I want to get started on it."

The operator took the wire, looked at it, and then glanced at Merritt dubiously.

Merritt leaned forward on his chair so that Holbrook could see him. He said, "I'd hold that order up for a few hours, Mr. Holbrook. That's good advice."

The storekeeper stared at him and then at the operator. He said slowly, "What's on, Ed?"

"I'd do it," Ed advised him. "Just a few hours one way or the other won't hurt, Mr. Holbrook."

"That's true," Holbrook murmured, but he was shaking his head doubtfully. "Ain't nobody tellin' me what it's all about?" he asked.

"Just a few hours," Merritt said. "You'll be saving yourself a lot of grief, Mr. Holbrook."

The storekeeper nodded. "I'll wait, Mr. Kane," he said, and he went out.

Merritt said, "A lot of wires like that? Orders for building supplies?"

"That's right," the operator said. "Past month or so. Plenty of them."

Merritt scowled. He sat there, looking at the

opposite wall, hearing riders coming into town, singly, in groups, hearing their talk in the road outside.

Footsteps went past the building once, and again the operator started to blink. The footsteps died away, and then they came again. The door opened, and Finn Tragan came in.

The operator was sitting at his instrument, his face a mottled color. Merritt sat in his chair, weight a little more forward now, ready to get up, but he didn't get up. He sat there, listening, watching the operator.

The operator said, "What can I do for you, Sheriff?"

"Reckon there's a message comin' through for Mr. Kane, Ed," Tragan said casually. "Thought I'd pick it up for him an' take it out. I'm goin' his way."

The operator picked up the wire from the pile on the top of his desk. He came over to the counter, set the paper down, and without a word turned and stepped through the rear door.

Merritt could see Tragan's shadow on the far wall. He watched the sheriff pick up the paper and stare at it, and then he came out of the chair, moving forward, hands at his side. He said gently, "Good news, Sheriff?"

Finn Tragan stared at him, an odd expression in his amber-colored eyes. His small hands rubbed his gun belt after he'd put the wire back on the counter, and he stood there, about six feet away from Merritt, with only the waist-high wooden counter between them. His eyes moved to Merritt's gun, and then he sniffed a little.

He said, "So you know somethin', Kane."

"Reckon I know a lot," Merritt nodded. "I know who shot down Tom Morse, too."

"Do you, now?" Tragan murmured. He took one short step backward, and he rubbed his nose with his left hand. He never took his eyes off Merritt.

"I know you're not Finn Tragan, but the El Paso Kid," Merritt continued easily, "and I know why West brought you here, Kid."

"You know a lot," the Kid smiled. "You know too much, Kane."

Merritt nodded. "Some things I can forget, Kid," he said softly. "I'm not forgetting Tom Morse."

"No?" the Kid said.

"No," Merritt smiled.

They stood there, and Merritt could hear a clock ticking on the shelf behind him. Up the street he could hear Jonathan West playing, softly, easily, the music seeming to hang in the air. A group of riders went by, and one of them whooped loudly.

"No," the El Paso Kid repeated. His eyes again moved to the paper on the counter, the first time they had left Merritt's face, and then his right hand moved, faster then Merritt Kane had ever

191

seen a hand move before. The Kid's gun came out of the holster as if by magic. The muzzle of it was lifting up above the rim of the counter when Merritt's first bullet hit him in the chest.

The Kid, a frail man, staggered back from the impact. It was as if he'd been hit in the chest with a heavy club. He reeled back toward the door, his mouth working, shoulders turned in a little. When he bounced against the doorsill, his hat fell off, and Merritt was surprised to see that his ash-blond hair extended only around the outer ridges of his hat. He was bald in the middle.

The Kid's gun roared twice, the bullets tearing through the wooden floor of the building, and then he went down, falling forward, landing on the side of his face and his right shoulder. Merritt was positive he was dead even before he hit the floor.

Reaching forward, Merritt picked up the telegraph message and placed it carefully in his shirt pocket after folding it up. He heard someone yelling up the street, and then the sound of running feet on the boardwalk.

He went out, pushing through the crowd that had started to gather. There were several Double Bell riders in the group, and then he saw Sabine Bell coming down the walk. He slowed down and he touched his hat when she came up.

She said one word. "Tragan?"

"That's right," Merritt nodded. "Come on with

me. You'll have to know about this, too." He took her by the arm, turned her around, and headed up toward the Wild West Saloon.

There were men standing on the porch of the Wild West, staring down toward the telegraph operator's office. Young Jonathan West was there, and Merritt looked up at him for a moment before going into the saloon. He frowned, not liking this part of it.

Merritt said to Sabine, "West around? Or Billy Deal, or Dunstan?"

"I just rode in," Sabine told him. "Why?"

Merritt took out the yellow telegrams. Inside, he motioned to Sam McGee, and the bouncer came over.

He said to McGee, "A hammer and a few nails, Sam."

McGee looked at him, and then at Sabine Bell. The Wild West was crowded already despite the early hour. Holbrook, the storekeeper, was up at the bar, chatting with several other Broken Bow businessmen. Holbrook looked at Merritt curiously.

McGee went behind the bar, bent down, and then came back in a few moments with a hammer and a box of nails. Merritt took them, walked to the side of the batwing doors, took out his two wires, and started to tack them to the wall.

Sabine Bell watched him. Then she moved closer to read the telegrams. Other men were

193

coming up, looking over her shoulder. The message on top read:

ADVISE IS GREAT KANSAS BUILDING
TO BROKEN BOW STOP INFORMATION
URGENT STOP WIRE

The message was addressed to the Great Kansas Railroad, Chicago, Illinois, and Merritt's name was on the bottom of it.

Below the first message was the reply that had come through that evening. It was from a man by the name of Johnson Ames, Great Kansas executive director. It read:

WHERE IS BROKEN BOW STOP WHO ARE
YOU STOP INFORMATION FALSE

Merritt had walked back to the bar and he was standing there, his elbows hooked over the wood, watching the crowd moving over to read the telegrams. Sabine Bell pushed out of the crowd, her face pale. She saw him at the bar and she came over, Sam McGee following her. McGee was rubbing his nose violently.

Sabine said quietly, "So it was all false—from the beginning."

"It was all false," Merritt nodded. "Somebody started the rumor and it built up."

"Stephen West started the rumor," Sabine said.

"The rumor started when he came to Broken Bow, and it started for a reason."

Sam McGee muttered, "What about the surveyors? What about this Mr. Dunstan?"

"The surveyors," Merritt said, "were fakes. A drunken man staggering through the Yellow Hills could have laid out as good a route. Dunstan is another fake. He doesn't represent Great Kansas. No one represents Great Kansas, because the railroad has no intention of coming here."

He could hear the murmur over at the wall. He saw Jim Holbrook, the storekeeper, come out of that crowd, his face sweating, eyes wild. Holbrook came over to Merritt. He gulped, "This can't be true, Mr. Kane."

"I'm afraid it is," Merritt told him. "This whole town has been duped."

"Fake surveyors," Sam McGee said. "Fake Great Kansas representatives, fake talk all around."

"A thousand dollars a foot," Holbrook was muttering. "One thousand dollars a foot, Mr. Kane!"

"I know," Merritt said.

"Stephen made a fortune out of this," Sabine Bell said grimly. "He's been buying for six months. He bought up a tremendous amount of real estate before this railroad talk even started."

"Reckon he's sold most of it by now," Merritt observed. He saw others coming away from those devastating wires on the wall. He recognized one of them as the gambler who'd intended to put up a huge gambling emporium in town. The gambler was a thin, pale-faced man with a black mustache and flashing black eyes. He came away from the wall, his face a sickly color, and he was swearing soundlessly, his lips moving, no words coming out.

There were others in the room, and as they stood at the bar more and more men crammed into the Wild West, the rumor having spread. Little knots of men gathered on the porch outside; they gathered inside the Wild West. They stood around Merritt, who had broken the story.

A man was yelling, "Git Sheriff Tragan."

Another man scowled. "Tragan's dead."

Merritt Kane said, "Tragan was in with them, with the surveyors, with West, with Dunstan, and with Asa Creel."

The crowd was getting ugly now. The talk became louder. Jonathan West had seen the messages too, and he came over to Merritt, his face miserable.

He said, "You're sure about this, Mr. Kane?"

Merritt looked at him. He said, "I'm sure about it, Jonathan. It would have happened sooner or later. They couldn't keep it covered up forever."

Jonathan nodded. He moved away through the crowd, and Merritt saw him go out through the door.

Sabine said quietly, "Merritt, this crowd is getting bad."

They could hear the noise out in the street because there was no more room inside the Wild West. There were women out there, too, women whose husbands had paid out heavy money for the choice lots on Main Street.

Holbrook seemed to be the center of activity. Holbrook, a big man with graying hair and hulking shoulders. Holbrook was on the porch, and Merritt could see his head over the batwing doors. Holbrook was sweating, his face still wild. He was saying loudly, "They can't get away with this—not in this town."

Sam McGee, from his corner of the bar, said to Merritt, "Everything was done legal-like, witnesses an' all. They have their deeds to the property, only the properties ain't worth a thousand dollars a foot."

A man on the porch yelled, "Get Dunstan down here. He's the man who's supposed to represent Great Kansas. Get him down here."

Part of the crowd surged away from the saloon, heading up toward the hotel.

McGee murmured, "Next thing, they'll be thinkin' about ropes." He glanced at Sabine Bell, and Sabine went pale.

Merritt didn't like it either, and he was wondering now if he'd been wise in lighting the fuse this way. It had to be done, because men like

Holbrook were getting themselves in deeper all the time. He hadn't expected this ugly turn the thing was taking. He'd expected righteous anger, but not force.

They went outside on the porch, and the crowd was still gathering. They were standing in the road, blocking all traffic. Then the crowd that had surged up to the hotel came back, but Dunstan was not with them. Instead they had a white-faced little man with a ratlike face. He was being dragged along reluctantly.

Sam McGee said, "Asa Creel's got himself into trouble this time, Merritt."

A man on the porch was shouting, "Creel was in with 'em. He sold me my lot on Main Street—a thousand a foot, too. Creel loaned Stephen West all kinds o' money when he came to this town. How about it, Asa?"

Creel was protesting feebly as they hauled him up on the porch and pushed him up against the two telegrams on the wall inside. Merritt heard him crying in a quavering voice, "I don't know anything about this, gentlemen. These were all business deals. I can't help it if the railroad isn't coming here."

Holbrook glared down at him. He said thickly, "You pay for hiring them surveyors, Asa? You pay this Dunstan chap to come here with his rotten lies?"

"I'm innocent," Creel protested. "I'm a banker,

gentlemen. I make loans. That's all I do."

"You were in the real-estate business, too, Creel," a man yelled from the porch, unable to get inside. "You sold me my lot, Creel. One thousand a foot."

The little gambler with the black eyes pushed through the crowd. He said tersely, "I'd say we have the wrong one, gentlemen. Mr. West is the man behind this whole business. Get West down here."

"Get West," another man nodded. "That's it."

They took up the cry, and it went outside to the street. "Get West—get West!"

Asa Creel was shoved aside roughly, and the crowd stormed outside into the street again. Merritt and Sabine Bell, standing near the door, were pushed along with them.

The shout was "West—we want West!"

A small man, breaking through the crowd, yelled, "You ain't gettin' West, boys. Stephen West, Dunstan, an' his sister rode off in one of our coaches an hour ago. They're headed north."

Merritt looked down at Sabine Bell. She stared up at him and said, "He's gone. It—it's better that way."

The crowd wasn't giving up so easily. Holbrook was yelling, "He's running off with half this town's money. He can't get away with that, boys!"

"All legal-like," Sam McGee murmured at

Merritt's elbow, but his voice was doubtful. He added, "But this crowd ain't worryin' about what's legal an' what's not."

"Let's get a posse organized," Holbrook roared. "We can catch up with that stage before it gets a dozen miles from here."

"A posse!" a man yelled.

The gambling man climbed up on one of the wicker chairs on the porch. He called sharply, "Boys, the sheriff of this town is dead. It seems he was as crooked as West and the others. We need the law behind us in order to organize a posse."

"What about this Deal chap?" Holbrook asked, and Merritt had been wondering about Handsome Billy Deal, too. Deal seemed to have vanished. He hadn't been with Tragan, and he didn't leave in the coach with West and Dunstan.

"Deal must have been as crooked as Tragan," the gambler scowled. "I vote we elect a new sheriff right now."

"Who?" Holbrook asked.

The gambler smiled coldly and pointed a finger straight at Merritt Kane, standing a dozen feet away from him. He said, "I vote we elect the man who cleaned up Cairo City, Abilene, Ellsworth, and Brisbane, the toughest and the squarest gun marshal in the West—Merritt Kane."

Merritt heard Sabine Bell gasp a little. She was looking up at him. He saw Jonathan West at the edge of the crowd, staring at him too, fear in his eyes. Jonathan West knew what this mob would do to Stephen West if it caught up with him. There would be no trial. It would be over in thirty minutes.

Holbrook was saying, "Gun marshal? That right?"

"I watched him work in Abilene," the gambler was saying. "I know him."

Merritt didn't say anything.

Holbrook called, "How about it, Kane? You want that job? We're goin' after Stephen West. It'll be legal then."

Merritt wanted to laugh. It was almost humorous. He'd come to Broken Bow for peace and quiet, and now they were offering him the star. There had been no peace, and there had been no quiet.

"Take it," Holbrook said tersely, "or we're goin' without a sheriff, Kane. You know what that means?"

Merritt knew what it meant. There was a tree waiting for Stephen West somewhere on the north road, a tree and a rope. He saw Jonathan West across the road, and then he heard Sabine Bell say quietly:

"A lynching would be an awful thing for this town, Merritt. We'd never live it down. If you can get Stephen back here to stand some kind of trial, it would be better."

Holbrook yelled hoarsely, "How many of you boys want Merritt Kane as sheriff of Broken Bow—the man who exposed the Great Kansas scheme?"

There was a roar of approval from the big crowd in the street, and then Merritt nodded.

He said briefly, "I'll take it, temporarily."

"Git Judge Bounce," a man howled. "Bring him up here."

Judge Bounce, a fat man with a wig, was whirled up through the crowd, his wig askew, sweating freely. In five minutes Merritt was sworn in and the star pinned to his vest. He looked down at it, and then rubbed the metal with his fingertips.

Holbrook said, "How many men you need in that posse, Sheriff?"

Merritt thought for a moment. "Dozen or two," he said. "You pick them out, Holbrook, and take them north on the stage road."

The storekeeper stared at him. "What about you, Kane?" he asked.

"I want to send a wire on ahead to Bolgerville," Merritt told him, "to hold up the coach when it comes through."

"Good," Holbrook nodded. He pushed away through the crowd, yelling.

Merritt went down the porch steps, Sabine with him, and Sam McGee went along also.

Sabine said, "I'm glad you took it, Merritt."

Behind them, as they walked toward the telegraph operator's shack, they could hear the noise dying down. Groups of men still stood around, talking excitedly, but they wanted justice now, not blood.

Holbrook's posse was mounted, hammering north across the bridge, up the slope, and out of the draw. Merritt stepped into the house, sent off his message, and came out again.

Jonathan West had joined Sam McGee and Sabine Bell outside. Young West said steadily, "I—I'd like to go along, Mr. Kane. Stephen's my brother. I want to be there."

Merritt looked at him. He said, "Your brother give you any idea where he was going?"

Jonathan shook his head. "He did say this afternoon that if he were suddenly called away from Broken Bow he'd get in touch with me later so that I would know where to meet him."

Merritt nodded. He was positive now that West had been ready to run for some time now. He'd probably sold most of his holdings and he had the cash with him. When he learned of the telegram, and realized that at least one man in Broken Bow suspected him, and that there might be more, he'd decided to pull out.

There was the matter of Tragan. The El Paso Kid had been the delaying action. The Kid was supposed to stop Merritt in one way or another, and probably rejoin Stephen West later. That left Handsome Billy Deal. Deal was not in town. Merritt was sure of that.

They went back up the street, and Sabine was saying, "I'm going along too, with some of my boys."

Merritt stopped. He said, "You know there might be trouble. You'd—"

"Stephen West was my fiancé," Sabine reminded him. "I want to go along, and you might need my boys."

"Posse's gettin' big again," Sam McGee murmured.

Sabine didn't wait for a reply. She stalked off to round up some of her riders.

McGee said, "I'll see if I can rent a horse, Merritt."

"Where are you going?" Merritt asked him.

"Thought I'd trot along with the posse," McGee told him.

"Why?" Merritt demanded.

McGee shrugged. "For the hell of it," he said honestly.

Merritt smiled a little. He paused at the hitching rack where he'd left the gray, and then he said to McGee, "What lies west of Broken Bow? What's the next town?"

McGee thought. "Ain't no town," he said. "Only Milltown, an' that ain't a town either."

"What's Milltown?" Merritt wanted to know.

"Fifteen miles due west," McGee told him. "Used to be a lumber mill there years ago, but it closed down. Couple of houses, a store, a saloon left. Shady characters stop in there when they want supplies an' don't like ridin' into an honest town."

Merritt nodded. "What's beyond Milltown?" he asked.

"Nothin'," McGee told him. "Open country."

Merritt thought about that, and the more he thought, the more he became convinced that he was right. Stephen West would have been a fool to think that he could escape on a slow-moving Concord coach. He had known that in a very short while the entire town would know about his crookedness, and that they might come after him. He'd had only an hour's start on them.

West knew that, and West undoubtedly had made different plans. He'd ridden out of Broken Bow on the northbound stage with Peter Dunstan and Fay. The chances were that Fay was Dunstan's wife and not his sister. The stage agent had sold him the tickets, letting the town know that he was leaving that way.

If someone with horses were waiting a few miles north of Broken Bow, Stephen West could leave the stage, with or without the Dunstans, and depart in a different direction. That would account for Handsome Billy Deal. Deal would be the man to bring up the spare mounts.

West, if he were not a fool, would head for California with his money. That meant he would pass through Milltown, undoubtedly stopping for supplies at that point.

Sabine Bell came up with her riders, five of them, and then Jonathan West walked a horse out of the livery stable.

Sabine said, "We're ready, Merritt."

Merritt stepped into the saddle. He said briefly, "Let's go."

Chapter Fourteen

BIG SAM MCGEE joined them as they clattered across the bridge and headed up out of the draw. Merritt could smell the dust lifted by Holbrook's posse, which had gone on ahead of them. The night was dark again, but they could see the road stretching out ahead of them, running parallel with the valley in which Merritt had seen the surveyors.

Merritt slowed down, bringing his horse to a walk, and Sabine, riding beside him, said curiously, "We won't catch them this way, Merritt."

"That's right," Merritt smiled faintly. "I don't think we'll catch them this way. We're moving west from here."

Sabine stared. "West?" she asked. "But the stage route is north."

"I don't believe Stephen West is on the stage any more," Merritt told her. "I feel that he skipped the stage, picked up horses he had waiting for him somewhere along here, and then headed west. He might stop at Milltown, and that's where we'll go looking for him."

Sam McGee had heard Merritt, and he was nodding vigorously. "Sounds right to me," he said. "West would be a damned fool to leave on a slow coach. If he has horses and he's headin' in another direction, throwin' the posse fifty miles off his trail, he's safe."

"So the posse is having a nice ride for itself," Sabine smiled, "in the wrong direction."

Merritt shrugged. "Reckon the ride will do them good," he murmured. "They'll cool off a little."

"You didn't want them in the first place, did you?" Sabine smiled.

"Never did like a posse around," Merritt stated. "They're usually shooting everything in sight, hitting everything but what they're aiming at. They're better off riding north. When they get back to Broken Bow they'll be tired, and tired men don't hang anybody."

Sam McGee laughed at that, and Merritt turned the party off the stage road, dipped down into the valley to the west, and then crossed the valley and the little stream that ran through it.

"What about Milltown?" Merritt asked Sabine Bell.

"I've seen it," Sabine told him briefly. "Not much to see. I remember one store owned by a man named Lorch. He's not popular with ranchers because he sells supplies to cattle rustlers and other shady characters back in the hills."

"If West needed supplies then," Merritt said, "he'd go to Lorch's."

"What about Miss Dunstan?" Sabine asked.

"Stephen wouldn't take her on an overland trip like that."

Merritt shook his head. "I think the Dunstans are still on the stage," he stated. "Stephen would have paid them off and they're in the clear. The posse knows West is the man who has the money."

"Posse might rough up that Dunstan chap a little," Sam McGee grinned, "but it wouldn't hurt him any."

Merritt glanced over at Jonathan West, riding a little to one side. Jonathan had said nothing since they'd started out. He'd been hit hard by the revelation that his brother was a crooked manipulator, and it would be a long time before the effect of it wore off.

A Double Bell hand, who knew the best route to Milltown, led the way, and they moved at a fairly fast pace when they reached the other side of the valley.

They went into timber a half hour after they'd left Broken Bow, and they followed an old corduroy road for about a mile or two before coming out into the open again. The land started to lift here, and the riding became more rough. They went down into deep draws, traversing them to the end, and then coming out in still rougher country.

At about midnight they had to make a long climb up a stiff grade, and reaching the top,

Merritt called a halt to give the horses a chance to blow. They dismounted and some of the men rolled cigarettes, squatting on their heels in the darkness.

Merritt could see their cigarette butts glowing as he stood beside Sabine Bell. Jonathan West had moved off by himself, and Merritt saw his slim figure outlined against the night sky.

Sabine said, "What about Fay Dunstan?"

"I don't believe she was Peter Dunstan's sister," Merritt said. "More likely his wife, or his lady friend." He added grimly, "I have no doubt now that she led me into an ambush this afternoon. She was in with them."

"I see," Sabine murmured.

Merritt glanced at her, but she said no more on the subject. In ten minutes they started to ride again, and it was still rough going through almost mountainous country now. They rode through woodland, the Double Bell rider following an almost indiscernible trail, and then they dipped into a canyon and scrambled across a cold stream in which the water came up to the horses' bellies.

On the other side of the stream the Double Bell man stopped his horse. Merritt said to him, "What's up?"

"Riders passed here," the Double Bell man said.

"How do you know?" Merritt asked him.

"Kin smell 'em," the man said laconically.

Merritt smelled the fresh horse droppings then, indicating that the riders had just passed by along this same trail.

Sam McGee said, "Looks like you were right, Merritt. They can't be too far ahead of us."

"How soon before we reach Milltown?" Merritt asked the Double Bell man.

"Another hour," the rider told him. "We're through the worst of it."

They came out on open range land again after having gone through these low mountains, and the riding was easier.

Sabine Bell said, "Milltown is right at the edge of the timber on the other side of this grade. You'll be able to see a light or two when we get to the top."

When they reached the top of the grade, Merritt called a halt. He could see a faint light like a star dead ahead of them, but it was too low to be a star.

The Double Bell rider said, "Milltown."

"You going to ride right in?" Sabine Bell asked.

Merritt shook his head. "If Deal is with him, there might be a fight," he said. "I'll have a look around myself first."

"So they'll take the shots at you first," Sabine murmured. "Is that the way it goes?"

Merritt smiled. "When you wear the star," he said, "you expect the shots, Miss Bell."

"What about my boys?" Sabine asked. "They expected to be in on this."

"Swing them around behind Milltown," Merritt advised. "If West tries to break out, he'll run right into you."

"You're going in there alone," Sabine said flatly. "What are you going to do, ask them to go back with you?"

Merritt shrugged. "Reckon I'll look around a bit," he said.

"You don't want any of my boys to get hurt," Sabine accused him. "That's the reason you're going in alone."

Merritt looked up at the night sky, and then at his horse's head. He said, "This is a posse, Miss Bell, under my command. I give the orders and I expect to have them obeyed. Now take your riders around behind Milltown and wait until you hear from me."

Sabine stared at him for a moment in a surprised silence, and Merritt could see that she was not accustomed to being spoken to like this. For a long time she had been giving the orders, running her own ranch. He could not see her face clearly in the darkness. It was a white blob before him. He heard her say almost contritely:

"We'll go. Be careful."

They moved away, a file of riders, Sabine in the lead now, all but one rider. Merritt pushed his horse over that way, and he said, "You, too, friend."

The rider was Jonathan West, and young West said, "My brother. I'm going in with you, Mr. Kane."

Merritt was silent for a moment, and then Jonathan said, "He might listen to me, Mr. Kane. I might be able to prevent trouble."

Merritt nodded, recognizing the fact that there was that chance. He said briefly, "I'm not looking for trouble, Jonathan, but I believe Billy Deal is in there, too, and Deal isn't the kind of man who will walk out with his hands up in the air—not to me, anyway."

Jonathan West didn't say anything. They sat there for a few moments, looking at that single speck of light ahead of them, and then Merritt said:

"We'll move up a little closer, and then go in on foot."

There was a breeze here blowing down from the timber behind Milltown. As they drew closer to the light they could see that the land rose abruptly behind the collection of shacks and tumble-down houses. This was probably new timber, Merritt was thinking, the new growth since Milltown had folded up.

Dismounting several hundred yards before they reached the first building, they started forward on foot. They'd lost the light they'd been following all the way in, but this was because another building had come into their line of vision.

It was quiet, so quiet that Merritt would have thought it was a ghost town, except that they'd seen the light, and they'd been following riders who had taken the same faint trail that they themselves had followed.

The wall of a building loomed up dead ahead of them, and they moved up into its shadow, standing there for a few moments. The roof of the building had fallen in, but the walls were still intact. Inside, Merritt heard a rat scurrying away. He looked around the corner of the building, and then he saw the light again, about fifty yards away now, down the single street, and the light came from a window.

Jonathan said softly, "That must be Lorch's store, Mr. Kane."

Merritt nodded. He could see the building, a long, low shed of a place with a sagging porch and a hitching rail out front. There were no horses at the rail, and Jonathan whispered:

"Maybe they went straight on. I don't see their horses."

"Horses could be in a shed in the back," Merritt told him. "They might even be staying until morning."

"What are you going to do?" Jonathan asked.

"Find the horses first," Merritt said. "Then we'll know."

They left the shadow of the tumble-down building and moved along to the next one, keeping behind the buildings along the street rather than walking on the street. There was a section of boardwalk running along one side, but most of it was rotted away. Weeds sprouted in the street. They passed a dozen buildings before they came up behind Lorch's, and more than half of the buildings had fallen in. Several of the others might have been occupied, but Merritt could not be sure. There were no lights at this hour of the night.

There was a stable behind the store, a stable that was little more than a long shed, open at one end. He could hear horses stamping inside the shed. He thought he heard voices inside the house, too, but he was not sure.

He said to Jonathan West, "Wait here. I'll have a look at the horses."

Moving in under the shadow of the shed, he waited until his eyes grew a little more accustomed to the light, and then he went down along the line of stalls. There were a half-dozen horses under the shed, which was large enough to accommodate two dozen.

As he went past each animal softly, quieting them, he rubbed a hand on their flanks. The last two animals at the far end of the shed were warm, indicating that they'd just been ridden. Merritt stood there for a few moments, positive now that his men were inside. Then he went back to Jonathan West.

He said succinctly, "They're inside. Two horses. Two riders."

Jonathan said, "Let me go in. I'll talk to him. I'll tell him we have this town surrounded and that he can't get out. I'll tell him he'll get a fair trial back in Broken Bow."

Merritt thought about that. If he went in himself, Billy Deal, if not Stephen West, would open up on him without giving him a chance to talk. They wouldn't shoot at young West, and there was a faint possibility that West would be reasonable about the matter.

"Tell them," Merritt said, "that our posse has this place surrounded so that a flea couldn't get through. Tell him we have a hundred men with us." He wondered after he said this how much money Stephen West had in his saddlebags in hard cash, and how much of a fight West would put up before he relinquished that money. Stephen West was not an easy loser, and he'd worked hard for that cash.

"I'll go in at the front," Jonathan said.

"You have a gun?" Merritt asked him suddenly.

"No."

Merritt nodded. "All the better," he said. "I'll be back here waiting. If they'll listen to reason, tell them to walk out into the street. You take their guns."

"He'll have to listen," Jonathan said doggedly.

Merritt didn't say anything. It was a long chance and he knew it, but it was a chance, and it might prevent bloodshed. He watched Jonathan move away from the edge of the shed, tall, thin in the darkness. Young West was about ten yards from the rear of the store building, starting to go around it to the front, when a rear door opened suddenly, yellow light flowing out across the back of the yard.

A tall man stood in the doorway, silhouetted against the light, and Merritt recognized him immediately as Handsome Billy Deal. Very smoothly Merritt lifted his Colt gun from the holster. Deal had seen West, and he was stiffening there in the doorway. His right hand dipped, and the gun came out of the holster.

Jonathan West had stopped at the outer edge of the lamplight. He said, "Mr. Deal—"

That was as far as he got. Deal's gun was swinging on the target when Merritt yelled loudly, "Deal—no!"

Billy Deal's gun roared, his first bullet going at Jonathan West, and West took it, lurched into the light, and went down on his knees, head sagging. Deal swiveled his gun toward the edge of the stable, and Merritt saw the orange flame dart out again. His own gun kicked slightly in his hand.

Deal was shooting at a shadow, but Merritt had his man silhouetted against the light. Deal knew

217

that, and he tried to move out into the shadows after he'd got off his second shot, which missed Merritt completely. Merritt's bullet caught him before he could make the quick jump.

Deal went down, but he was still in the fight. On hands and knees just outside the patch of light, he fired again at Merritt, lifting himself a little to get off the shot, firing wildly again because he'd been hit now and his sense of direction was bad.

Merritt, walking forward, released the hammer again. Deal pitched upward and forward. He went down on his face. Merritt stopped, still outside the light. He stood there for a moment. Then the light went out as the lamp was smashed inside the house. He held the gun lined on the doorway, knowing that someone was there just to the side of the doorpost, waiting, watching.

Stephen West's voice came at him: "That you, Kane?"

Merritt said, "That damn fool Deal just got your brother, West. He's lying out here."

Horses were coming in. He could hear them hammering up the street, coming toward Lorch's—Double Bell riders. Then he heard something else inside the house, by the door. It was Stephen West—cursing steadily, slowly, the cursing ending in a kind of sob. Then West's gun boomed, and Merritt felt the tug of the bullet as it went through his coat.

He fired four times at the flash of West's gun,

218

one shot following the other so fast that they could hardly be counted. He held the empty gun in his hand, hearing a man staggering around inside the house, hearing him fall.

Out front Sabine Bell was calling, "Merritt! Merritt!" There was a kind of fear in her voice.

Merritt reloaded, and he called, "Back here."

A man inside the house was saying, "I ain't in this, gents. These boys wanted supplies. That's all I know."

"Strike a light, Lorch," Merritt ordered.

He went up to Jonathan West, knelt down beside him, and he was still there when the lamp went on and Sabine Bell reached him. He said briefly, "Deal shot him down. He was trigger-crazy."

Jonathan was still alive. The bullet had gone through his right side. He was still conscious, breathing heavily. He gasped, "He—he wouldn't come, Merritt."

"No," Merritt said, "he wouldn't come."

The storekeeper, Lorch, a short, squat, barrel-chested man, held the lamp so that they could see. He said, "There's a dead one in there, mister."

Merritt looked down into Jonathan West's eyes. Young West closed his eyes for a moment and then opened them again. He said softly, "All right. All right, Mr. Kane."

Merritt said to one of the Double Bell riders, "Find those saddlebags in the house. Then one of you boys ride back to Broken Bow and bring Doc Barker out with you."

They got Jonathan into the house and placed him on a cot. Merritt washed the wound, noticing that the bullet had gone clean through, which was very good.

Sabine said to Merritt, "Doc Barker won't get here till morning."

Merritt nodded. "He'll be all right," he said, nodding toward Jonathan West on the cot. "We might be able to move him in a buckboard in a few days."

"We'll take him to our place," Sabine said. "Roxy can look after him."

Merritt went outside. He stood there in the darkness at the rear of the house, and then he rolled a cigarette. He said to Sabine, "What'll he do now that his brother's gone?"

"Roxy tells me they're getting married," Sabine said. "He wants to go east and see if he can get playing engagements."

Merritt nodded. He didn't say anything for a few moments, and then he murmured, "How do you feel?"

She knew what he meant. She said, "All right. I'm sorry it happened this way."

"They'll get their money back in Broken Bow," Merritt observed. "It'll be a quiet town again. No railroad." He liked to think of it that way. It was a great load off his mind. The dream was coming true after all. He remembered that his money was nearly gone, that his ranchhouse had been burned down and his stock destroyed, but Broken Bow was the same. He was going to settle down here. He had nice neighbors!

Big Sam McGee loomed up out of the darkness. He said to Merritt, "That Lorch fellow has a pretty good stock of liquor back there, Merritt. I'm thinkin' after what you've been through you could stand—" He stopped, noticing Sabine Bell on the other side of the doorway. He said, "Hell. Didn't want to butt in here." He backed away, and Merritt said to him:

"You're not butting in, Sam."

Sabine Bell's voice came out of the shadows, a hint of laughter in it. She said, "Sure you are, Sam."

Sam McGee chuckled. He kept moving away, and he called back, "Lady's always right, Merritt. You'll find that out."

Merritt Kane lighted his cigarette. In the yellow glow of the match he saw Sabine Bell's face. She was smiling at him. The match went out, and Merritt said softly, "It was a good dream."

Books are produced in the United States using U.S.-based materials

Books are printed using a revolutionary new process called THINKtech™ that lowers energy usage by 70% and increases overall quality

Books are durable and flexible because of Smyth-sewing

Paper is sourced using environmentally responsible foresting methods and the paper is acid-free

Center Point Large Print
600 Brooks Road / PO Box 1
Thorndike, ME 04986-0001 USA

(207) 568-3717

US & Canada:
1 800 929-9108
www.centerpointlargeprint.com